W9-BRJ-141

GOD CAME TO MY GARAGE SALE

Dr. Marni Hill Foderaro

Copyright © 2019 Dr. Marni Hill Foderaro.

All rights reserved. No part of this book may be used or reproduced by any means, graphic, electronic, or mechanical, including photocopying, recording, taping or by any information storage retrieval system without the written permission of the author except in the case of brief quotations embodied in critical articles and reviews.

This is a work of fiction. All of the characters, names, incidents, organizations, and dialogue in this novel are either the products of the author's imagination or are used fictitiously.

Balboa Press books may be ordered through booksellers or by contacting:

Balboa Press
A Division of Hay House
1663 Liberty Drive
Bloomington, IN 47403
www.balboapress.com
1 (877) 407-4847

Because of the dynamic nature of the Internet, any web addresses or links contained in this book may have changed since publication and may no longer be valid. The views expressed in this work are solely those of the author and do not necessarily reflect the views of the publisher, and the publisher hereby disclaims any responsibility for them.

The author of this book does not dispense medical advice or prescribe the use of any technique as a form of treatment for physical, emotional, or medical problems without the advice of a physician, either directly or indirectly. The intent of the author is only to offer information of a general nature to help you in your quest for emotional and spiritual well-being. In the event you use any of the information in this book for yourself, which is your constitutional right, the author and the publisher assume no responsibility for your actions.

Any people depicted in stock imagery provided by Getty Images are models, and such images are being used for illustrative purposes only.
Certain stock imagery © Getty Images.

Print information available on the last page.

ISBN: 978-1-9822-3475-1 (sc)
ISBN: 978-1-9822-3476-8 (e)

Balboa Press rev. date: 10/10/2019

CONTENTS

AUTHOR BIOGRAPHY

Dr. Marni Hill Foderaro is an award-winning educator and celebrated author. She earned her doctorate in education and completed postdoctoral studies at Harvard after a very successful and rewarding 35-year career as a high school special education teacher. Marni is a lover of animals, nature, music and world travel. She values honesty, integrity, equality and goodness and prays for peace on earth. She was born in the South, raised her children in the Midwest and has made the Caribbean her home.

www.godcametomygaragesale.com

"God Came To My Garage Sale is an outstanding and inspirational triumph! Filled with relatable synchronicities, Dr. Marni Hill Foderaro thoughtfully guides the reader on an insightful journey towards spiritual awareness and meaningful self actualization — illustrating the importance of staying in Peace and using Love to handle life's challenges."

James Redfield, Bestselling author of THE CELESTINE PROPHECY series of books

"A remarkable account of the Spiritual experiences of one woman that can inspire us all to grow, learn, and open our hearts. Very moving!"

Thomas John, Psychic Medium and Author of Never Argue with a Dead Person: True and Unbelievable Stories from the Other Side, Host of Seatbelt Psychic

"God Came To My Garage Sale is such a lovely, feel-good book and Marni perfectly captures the challenges we face with our own Spirituality and our need to be open to Spirit. This is a great insight into life after death."

Lisa Williams, Psychic Medium, Author, Speaker, Teacher

"Spiritual awakenings can happen anywhere, at anytime, to anyone and usually when one least expects it. Quite often it is as a result of living through life's all too real hardships that people find their inspirational truths and clarity. The questions aren't: does God exist and where is He or She? The question is: are you open to experiencing and having a loving relationship with God and Spirit? Dr. Marni Hill Foderaro brilliantly takes the reader on a journey of truth and clarity through relatable scenarios of everyday life that we, the reader, can totally, easily and personally connect with. Thought provoking and challenging insights are the readers' reward in this literary find entitled: God Came To My Garage Sale."

Christopher Stillar, Canadian Psychic Medium, Author of Pennies from Heaven: A Medium's Two Cents on Life and Death

"Our loved ones in Spirit are always sending us signs. You don't have to believe or be religious to relate to everyday encounters of the Divine. God Came To My Garage Sale is a must-read for anyone seeking truths and answers to questions about life after death. The world will soon realize that the veil is being lifted and our Conscious Collective is moving toward peace, love and unity. Dr. Marni Hill Foderaro, through her character's honesty, strength, insight and open awareness very positively and eloquently articulates that Divine light comes out of earthly darkness, hardships and challenges, and that Spiritual synchronicities exist through the relatable common. As an evidentiary Psychic Medium who has been honored to provide thousands of accurate readings to those in various stages of belief and grief, I can attest that the Spiritual signs described in this moving book are the 'real deal.' I commend Marni on her ability to guide the reader as they embark on their own awakening journey while reading every Spiritual scenario in this amazing inspirational fiction novel. It is not a coincidence that you have been drawn to read God Came To My Garage Sale. Prepare to be illuminated in the revelation that our loved ones are always near."

Lea Mittel, Michigan-based evidentiary Psychic
Medium of truemediumreadings.com

"Near-Death Experiences, Out-of-Body Events, After-Death Communications, Mystical Miracles!! Today, people the world o'er are having weird and transformative encounters they often don't understand. Spiritual leaders declare 'The veil is thinning', scientists conduct research into deeper consciousness and black holes, and Dr. Marni Hill Foderaro brings these truly divine and life-altering experiences home to our modern American middle-class existence, sensitizing us about what to watch for and what it all means. This amazing and inspirational book is an enlightening manual for learning about the loving world we came from and how we are connected to it and each other."

Diane Willis, Founder and President of Chicago IANDS
(International Association for Near Death Studies),
Native American Flutist, Spiritual Counselor.

"When it comes to God and the Universe, I am a firm believer in meaning for everything, which is the opposite of reason for everything. Every human life experience may not have a reason, but looking deeper into the hidden messages that God and the Universe bring to us, you will see that there will always be meaning in every message and every encounter. Dr. Marni Hill Foderaro and I have had that very similar encounter: Finding each other at the perfect time in our personal lives and career paths. As Marni and I have grown through our working relationship, we have come to realize the meaning in our own personal experiences and why each of us were meant to meet and be in each other's lives. In her first novel, God Came To My Garage Sale, Marni eloquently portrays the synchronicity with God and the Universe. You will find yourself having similar connections with miracles. This book is truly enlightening and inspiring. The Spiritual scenarios are derived from the character's personal encounters and are translated into literary form as an outstanding work of inspirational fiction, with relatable stories that are transformational, fun and exciting to read."

Michelle "Motherella" Piper, Ph.D., Psychic Medium, Spiritual Influencer, Author

"God Came To My Garage Sale is an uplifting, fun and inspirational novel to read. Marni does a great job of introducing Spiritual wisdom that the reader can relate to while taking you on a thoughtful and heartfelt journey. This book will open your heart and mind to the world of Spirit."

Jill Kempner, Angel Professional, Coach, Teacher

"What a great story about how the Spirit World is always near. Our loved ones never die! An extraordinary collection of events meant to inspire and uplift us. You just never know who will show up at your garage sale!"

Julie Adreani, Minister of Angels, Certified Spirit Medium

One Spiritual event or Divine encounter happened after another at Janet's garage sale. The connections and gradual realization regarding the inaccuracy of what she was taught to believe about life and death presented themselves like slow leaks of water from a broken faucet; little by little these drips transformed into tears that released a torrent that flooded Janet's mind, body and soul. She had a significant Spiritual Awakening that was previously held back by a dam of sorts, about the truth regarding our existence in this three-dimensional world called "earth." Who knew that the power to go beyond this earthly plane actually lies within each of us? Who knew that we could manifest our realities to attain a deeper and more Spiritual understanding? Who knew that God could come to an ordinary garage sale?

I lovingly dedicate this book to my wonderful and supportive life partner Rick. I wrote this book with sincere gratitude to God, guidance from Angels and my Spirit Guides and blessings from my family and friends, here on earth and in alternate energy dimensions.

FOREWORD

"The magnificent and awesome truth that our consciousness survives death and the importance of focusing our earthly efforts on love and positive interactions throughout our lifetime has been voiced by the millions of people who have experienced death and have subsequently survived over the centuries, but increasingly so as resuscitation efforts improved. Near-Death Experiencers and individuals who have had Spiritually Transformative Encounters the world over, like Dr. Marni Hill Foderaro, are bravely speaking out to share their riveting, uplifting and life-altering accounts, so that the veil will become more transparent and humanity will learn to transform their lives toward love and goodwill to all, and to present the world with an offering of peace.

This beautiful and inspirational fictional book is a gift to the reader, filled with the character's firsthand accounts of Spiritual miracles, Divine encounters and metamorphic awareness leading to growth and self-actualization. God Came To My Garage Sale will definitely assist you with finding a more positive path in your life and will give you insight into what lies ahead for all of us after the veil is lifted!"

Barbara Bartolome
2X NDEr, Speaker, Founder/Director of IANDS (International Association for Near Death Studies) Santa Barbara, Board Member of NDERF (Near Death Experience Research Foundation)

INTRODUCTION

"Ignorance is the curse of God; knowledge is the wing where with we fly to heaven."

William Shakespeare

Janet Smith, who raised her family in the comfort and structure of Westfield, Indiana, a suburb of Indianapolis, is forced to conduct what she hopes is her final garage sale. As she begins the process of physically shedding the extensive material remains of her accumulated memories, hopes and dreams, practically giving away treasures of the past she held onto with the intent of future utility, she could feel the expansive void in her supposedly coveted perfect life. Forging through the piles of her collected belongings, ranging from everyday household items and travel treasures to significant vintage heirlooms, she grieves so many losses: the break up of her family unit, even though it was by her choice; her financial stability, equity and credit; and her dream home complete with the white picket fence, pool and garden. This catastrophic culmination of life changes that contributed to what should have been an ordinary, non-eventful summer garage sale, was anything but.

Janet knew that her decisions would mean a change in her advantageous lifestyle. Even though her life would drastically alter, she had a positive outlook and hope for her future. She was accepting of the inevitable loss of all of the acquired material comforts she was accustomed to if it meant taking the first steps necessary to walk the road to freedom, safety, happiness and self-actualization as she embarked on her healing journey. The garage sale had to happen, even though she had promised herself she would never again subject herself to the humility of collecting pocket change as she practically gave away items that were once meaningful, useful and monetarily worth a great deal more than she could ever recoup. Janet had no choice but to significantly downsize to a small rental apartment in Carmel, the next town over, because her substantial 7,000 square foot upscale home was in foreclosure. Janet now needed to somehow salvage any money she could just to make ends meet, hence, the garage sale. Out of darkness, however, eventually came light. The garage sale she initially dreaded turned out to be the most beautiful and positive experience of Janet's life. Little did she know that she was about to embark on Spiritually Transformative Encounters that would forever change her thoughts about life, death and the afterlife.

One Spiritual event or Divine encounter happened after another at Janet's garage sale. The gradual connection and realization of the inaccuracy regarding what she was taught to believe about life and death presented themselves like slow leaks of water from a broken faucet; little by little these drips transformed into tears that released a torrent that flooded Janet's mind, body and soul. She had a significant Spiritual Awakening that was previously held back by a dam of sorts, about the truth regarding our existence in this three-dimensional world called "earth." Who knew that the power to go beyond this earthly plane actually lies within each of us? Who knew that we could manifest our realities to attain a deeper and more Spiritual understanding? Who knew that God could come to an ordinary garage sale?

This garage sale was the catalyst for a life-changing, evidentiary Spiritual Awakening that opened up Janet's world to the true reality that our departed loved ones have not really left us; they are still very much "alive." This garage sale also brought with it amazing events that encouraged and prompted Janet to experience a great deal of reflection and healing. At the time she didn't know that, in fact, our world's Conscious Collective was simultaneously entering an era of major transformation. Janet would soon find out that the often painful and negative trials and tribulations endured as a result of illnesses, accidents and malicious human interactions on this earthly plane are actually karmic lessons of our journey that we sign up to experience and learn from as part of our souls' contracts. We feel that we are humans having a Spiritual experience, when in fact we are Spiritual beings having a human experience. Despite the aftermath she found herself in, Janet's soul was naturally and instinctively saturated with peace, love, light, forgiveness, acceptance and more happiness than she had ever experienced before. She was always an empathetic, positive and loving soul. Yes, she was currently in survival mode, but instead of hurt, anger, vindictiveness or despair, she had an overwhelming sense of calm and hope for her future.

Every person that came by and all of the events that happened at Janet's garage sale on that early Saturday morning in July brought with them a mystical lesson for her to experience and absorb. Each Divine exposure was significantly Spiritual and was collectively instrumental in positively transforming Janet's life forever. Each person and engagement brought a message of love and healing to spark the flame within her to search for the truth and answer the age-old questions she had always had, which were "What happens when we die?" and "Is there more to this life on earth than what we think?" There were no barriers for Janet as she began surprisingly accessing and being gradually shown this miraculous Spiritual realm; her experiences felt just as real as any grounded, earthly experiences she had ever encountered. The only difference she could discern was that time seemed to slow way down or didn't even exist at all; an interaction that really couldn't have been more than a few seconds in earth-time felt like very long, drawn-out, slow-motion minutes or hours if she could even find the words to quantify them.

There were many that came to Janet's garage sale, however there were certain seemingly ordinary people followed by mystical events that she experienced in a transcendental way that made such an impact that they changed her worldview and led her to the burning question: "Did God come to my garage sale?" At one point she was surrounded by hundreds of dragonflies that felt like a swarm of connected generational souls engulfing her with love, peace and reassurance. She was reminded of her prayers to Saint Gerard being answered with confirmation coming in the form of a license plate name on a speeding yellow corvette. She was graced by the presence of an old man dressed in all white who was the spitting image of a favorite childhood school teacher and who seemed to disappear into thin air after a connection with her brother's pet dog. There were many more significant events that included the commonly-referenced and well-documented signs from Heaven such as pennies, feathers, red cardinals, orbs, distinctive and familiar smells, music, visitations, electronic interference and repeating numbers. All of these unbelievable people and miraculous events from the garage sale led Janet on a transformative Spiritual Awakening journey prompting her to begin practicing mindful meditation, attending workshops on NDEs-Near Death Experiences, reading numerous books on transcendental enlightenment, watching countless YouTube vlogs with first-hand testimonials and consulting with gifted psychic mediums and energy healers.

Carl Jung alluded to the Collective Unconscious where there is an energy source that surrounds us all and contains the memories of the entire human race; maybe that was at play at this particular garage sale. Authors and worldwide symposium lecturers and facilitators Eben Alexander, the former Harvard Medical School neurosurgeon who in 2008 had one of the most documented and scientifically studied NDEs, and his life partner Karen Newell, the cofounder of Sacred Acoustics who mixes audio binaural beats, attest to a shift in the experiences and consciousnesses of people on earth where they affirm that more and more individuals, like Janet, are activating their heart centers and embarking on the transformative process of changing from being stubborn skeptics to enthusiastic believers with regards to accepting and embracing the universally Divine Heaven dimension. The famous theoretical physicist and intellect Albert Einstein, who received the 1921 Nobel Prize, proposed the theory of relativity, developed the speed of light formula of E=mc2, and wrote over 1,400 letters now housed at the Hebrew University in Jerusalem, Israel believed that there exists an extremely powerful unseen force and energy phenomenon of Love that science and mankind are not able to harness. Someone once wrote, "After the failure of humanity in the use and control of the other forces of the universe that have turned against us, it is urgent that we nourish ourselves with another kind of energy if we want our species to survive, if we are to find meaning in life, if we want to save the world and every sentient being that inhabits it. Love is the one and only answer. Perhaps we are not yet ready to make a bomb of love, a device powerful enough to entirely destroy the hate, selfishness and greed that devastate the planet. However, each individual carries within them a small, but powerful generator of love whose energy is waiting to be released. When we learn to give and receive this universal energy, we will have affirmed that love conquers all, is able to transcend everything and anything, because love is the quintessence of life." James Redfield, the best selling author of The Celestine Prophecy series, who continues to tour the globe inspiring people to actualize their goals, energize their lives by living peacefully and reflecting on insights for higher Spiritual Awareness, notes that there is a cross-generational awareness happening right now. Tamara Gerstemeier-Sweeney, a worldwide advocate whose mission is to provide extensive support to parents and children unfortunate enough to suffer narcissistic abuse, injustice in our family court system and extreme Parental Alienation, is the founder of a nonprofit organization 501(c)(3) charity whose title says it all: "Love Dominates." She advocates to choose love over hate and compassion over judgment. That is what we all should do.

Reflecting on her newfound and mind-opening awareness that there is more to this earthly life than she originally thought, Janet Smith searched deep within her consciousness for answers to questions, so many questions. As an Atheist, more as a result of her upbringing as opposed to her own personal discovery and choice, Janet had previously struggled to accept or embrace organized religion. Eventually converting to Catholicism as an adult, she began to get involved in the church and its rituals, even becoming a regular Lector at her local parish. When Janet would pause to really reflect, question and contemplate what purpose everything had in the world and what this earthly life was all about, such as our existence and how humans correlate with the grand scheme of the universe, she could only focus so long on this topic before the busy responsibilities and routines of "life" took over. After her garage sale and her resulting amazing, transformational and miraculous experiences, she wholeheartedly embraced the concept that there are no coincidences, encounters are synchronistically orchestrated by Divine intervention and "everything happens for a reason." Even though it sounded cliche to her, she was sure that there were higher purposes and God-like forces at work, and that most likely, brought on by her traumatic life change and resulting garage sale experiences and encounters, she was finally ready to be enlightened, exposed to and to accept the bigger picture.

Without a shred of doubt, Janet just knew that God came to her garage sale.

CHAPTER 1

Dancing Dragonflies

"Our prayers should be for blessings in general, for God knows best what is good for us."

Socrates

The swarm of dragonflies surrounded me. I remember distinctly feeling that somehow these hundreds of dragonflies were engulfing me in warm, supportive and loving protection as I reflected that life as I knew it was falling apart in front of me. It was as if each dragonfly, big, medium and small, represented many lifetimes of ancestors, my ancestors, coming together at this critical watershed moment in my life, so as to give me strength during this dreaded garage sale weekend. I didn't think anyone would believe me when I told them about what happened with these dragonflies, so luckily at some point during the event I knew to pull out my iphone and was able to video record at least half of the experience for proof. Wow! What an experience it was! It was a sunny Saturday morning in July. I had painstakingly worked many weeks preparing for the garage sale, sorting through boxes and arbitrarily assessing value to each item and affixing on a price label. I had already felt like I put in a full day's work, even though it was only 7:30 in the morning. I'm not sure what prompted me, but I chose to take a sentimental reflection break and stroll out to my cul-de-sac island, the one I maintained for 20 years with seasonal plantings and a bench I had assembled and kept looking fresh with a yearly coat of wood stain. I turned to say goodbye and take a hard, long look at my beautiful home. This was the home of my dreams, down to the hunter green awnings, symmetrical window boxes overflowing with colorful, cascading flowers, gorgeous pool, inviting wraparound porch and swing, gazebo, gingerbread accents and of course the quintessential white picket fence. It was also the home of my dreams because there were so many wonderful memories with my children contained within the walls of each expansive room. I was usually on-the-go and kept myself busy and productive, but a feeling stronger than me caused me to halt then and there and really take in the house, a structure which represented my entire world, my fairytale; a story being abruptly rewritten and which was crumbling to pieces. I was awestruck and stunned as I saw an individual dragonfly and then groups of dragonflies descend and swarm upon me in the center cul-de-sac island in front of my house. Time most definitely slowed to a steady and constant hum. I remember watching the first very large dragonfly slowly swoop down in front of me as if to say, "It's all going to be O.K." Soon after, more dragonflies appeared out of nowhere. There were at least five of them at this point. I stood still and was in awe. I've always appreciated nature and living creations in all forms, including insects. Well, there is one exception: I hate mosquitos. Mosquitos have always seem to gravitate towards me and cause me great discomfort with bites, welts and itching. I noticed the specific details and realized that these five dragonflies were of varying sizes: one very big one, the first one I saw, and then others a bit smaller with one even appearing to be a baby. I felt like I was being surrounded by a family. The feeling I had was of confirmation, safety, peace and love. Unconditional love. Inside my heart at that very moment I was reassured somehow by these five dragonflies that I would survive this life change. Whatever I would need would be provided for me. I distinctly remember feeling the heart center of each dragonfly. Then all of a sudden hundreds of dragonflies descended on the cul-de-sac and circled around me. It was clear to me that somehow these dragonflies were all part of my own soul group and were uniting in a team effort of sorts. Just before the dragonflies made their coordinated effort to wrap their love around me, I was feeling a bit melancholy. I knew that I really shouldn't feel victimized and be so hard on myself, especially since I chose to embark on this life change. I was exhausted from preparing for this mega garage sale, but knew I needed to do this. I was actually very lucky that I eventually made the decision and had the strength to pursue a better and more positive path to my life.

History shows that people don't readily accept all sorts of changes or progressive initiatives, even when they are assured that the resulting outcome will be positive and beneficial. Even the great geniuses of the world who had remarkable, innovative and unbelievably progressive ideas, most of which were proven true many years later by modern science, were discounted and forced to live their lives without support and were void of truthful confirmations. Some were scorned, sentenced to death or had their life cut short by righteous gangs of non-believers. Galileo's discovery of the moons of Jupiter and the concept of gravity were met by refusal to accept or incorporate these ideas into the societal belief system of the evolving world at that time. Our modern commonwealth currently lives in an evidentiary, must-have-scientific-proof existence. Very little teaching and acceptance of the Spiritual realm and encounters exists today, although there is an upward trend to embrace the thought that there is a universal shift in the relationship of Spirituality and mankind currently gaining widespread acknowledgement. There is most definitely a Spiritual Awakening of the Collective Consciousness. The mysteries of life after death continue to be unexplained phenomena in academic and scientific circles. But thanks to the easy availability of technology, the global exposure and openness to the general public regarding varying points of view, the organization IANDS-the International Association for Near Death Studies is able to broadcast hundreds and hundreds of testimonials and personal firsthand accounts of ordinary people's miraculous Divine experiences confirming that people really don't die and that we are really Spiritual souls having a human experience. There truly seems to be a much higher purpose to our life on earth. I was just now finding this out on this July weekend as I was unloading and discarding the material remains of my collected life.

My garage sale was larger than most in my neighborhood. I had very little cash flow to pay for my bills, my living expenses, the utilities and the back, unpaid property taxes for such a big house. In fact it was a challenge just to keep food on the table. I went from living the "American Dream" and a "fairytale" life to finding out that I was actually existing in a false reality, and had been for decades. My change in life circumstances reminded me of a huge financial now-you-have-it now-you-don't scandal of a well-known, well-respected businessman when I was a tween growing up in the small Midwest town of Bloomfield, Indiana. The 1960's scandal involved the longtime owner of our town's only children's toy store. The store was called "The Wonder Shop" and kids of all ages loved to frequent it, especially on weekends. Not only was it jam-packed with every toy ever imagined, the store housed a colorful and well-stocked aquarium in the back and each child that came into the store on a Saturday got a helium balloon, whether they made a purchase or not. Just like many of my neighborhood friends and childhood classmates, I went there mainly to see the fish and get a balloon. We didn't own an aquarium and none of my friends or neighbors did either. If we wanted to see real live fish we would have to go to the Indianapolis Zoo and see the Mystic Marine Life Aquarium. Oh yeah, once a year there was a local Bloomfield Days fair we called "The Jamboree" where my brothers and I would play quarter carnival games at various booths. My favorite game was the one where you could win goldfish if you were able to accurately toss a ping pong ball into a small jar that was filled with water and a goldfish. I often guessed that not many goldfish actually survived after coming home from the carnival. The Wonder Shop owner's wife was shocked, just as I was after decades, to learn that the financial success she thought she had attained was not grounded in reality. She was a business person in her own right and managed the town's children's upscale boutique clothing store. When I went to The Wonder Shop, I always chose a red balloon.

I was partial to red balloons after my parents arranged for me to participate in a pantomime play when I was six years old. I had the part of the young girl who walked across the stage toting a blue balloon, capturing the attention of the red balloon. This play was performed by a group of theater students who were in the drama department of the college my dad taught at. It was a silent play and a spinoff of the original, Academy

Award-winning short French film/screenplay "The Red Balloon" by Albert Lamorisse. The storyline very cleverly captures the adventures of a young lad who develops a relationship with a sentient balloon. This red balloon went with him everywhere, whether it was to school, church, the market or the playground. I remember watching this film many times over the years. The plot always got tense when it came to the chase scene where the boy, with his human-like balloon flying just above him and following him through the streets of Paris, France, was being chased by a gang of older boys whose mission was to pop the balloon, essentially "killing" it. One of my favorite childhood Christmas gifts, besides my Easy Bake Oven, trolls and nurse's dress up costume, was receiving the oversized book of the Red Balloon film so I could relive each moment in print. The photographs in the book were actual photos that were taken during the filming of the movie. The book ended up receiving the New York Times Best Illustrated Children's Book of the Year. As a nurse I hosted an annual reading day at the hospital. I would surprise the kids and create interest with a special red helium balloon when I would enter young patients' rooms, getting the children's attention before I would read from the book. It was such a departure from the video games and "educational" electronics that the kids were used to. I still marvel about the film's magical ending scene where hundreds of balloons of various sizes and colors fly though the air from the different neighborhoods of Paris, all to unite with and provide hope to the boy who is mourning the loss of his red balloon. The hundreds of the red balloons' anthropomorphic counterparts collectively banded together to carry him off high into the sky above the Paris rooftops. There is such an uncanny similarity of the balloons to the dragonfly experience I had. Even though I still own the original and worn out book that my parents gave me, I recently went on online and found that Half-Price Books was selling the French version of the book and I was compelled to purchase it. Here I'm buying something else that I really don't need while I'm trying to sell everything else.

The town's clothing store was the only one that specifically catered to children. It was called "The Youngster's Shop," however all the locals called it "Janet's" after the manager's name. My parents never bought us clothes from Janet's because they were too expensive. Even though I never shopped there or got clothes from The Youngster's Shop, I had a special connection to the store because the store's name was the same as my name. I worked hard during middle and high school babysitting and cleaning houses so that I could get clothes-money to save up for the annual First Presbyterian Church rummage sale; that is where my wardrobe came from. I knew my friends knew that my clothes were all second-hand, but none of my peers ever said anything negative to me. I would have loved to have gotten my cousins' old clothes, but even though we were fairly close in age and size, they lived too far away and we didn't see them often enough for me to get their hand-me-downs. Actually, I really liked rummage sale and garage sale clothes. Even to this day, those are the clothes I prefer. My favorite shopping venues are Goodwill, Savers, The Salvation Army or garage sales. Not only can I find great stuff and the price is right, I don't feel bad if I get a stain or a tear and have to discard an item. Some local Indiana historian created this amazing diorama of The Youngster's Shop in the 1970's and presented it as a gift to the owners for the store's 10th Anniversary. It was made with such attention to detail. This diorama was proudly displayed in the storefront window until 2001 when it was eventually donated to the Bloomfield Historical Society for future generations to enjoy.

I needed to have this garage sale, not only to downsize and declutter, but to make ends meet and continue to make good on and chip away at my newfound and unexpected financial obligations. Silly me, at first I was under the impression that I could keep and live in my dream house. I should have methodically reviewed our family's financial accounts over the years so that I would not have had to experience the shock of the monetary devastation in which I found myself in. But that would have meant I wouldn't have had this garage sale on this particular July weekend and I may not have experienced all that I did that steered my life on this amazing Spiritual course. I've heard it said that "God works in mysterious ways." Like what happens during most garage sales, it seemed the customer traffic came in waves. It was during this first big lull in activity that the harsh reality of my losses hit me. I walked around my stuffed-to-capacity four-car garage and adjoining oversized driveway, which was scattered with collections, housewares, clothes, sports equipment, tools, books and knickknacks that now seemed such a waste of money. I wanted and needed to recoup some of that money. I longed for this garage sale to be over and I knew it was necessary to stick it out. I had thought about just calling a charity for a donation pick up or even hiring 1-800-got-junk to take it all away in one fell swoop, but I not only needed whatever money I could get, later on it was clear that I also needed to face the reality of the fact that in my attempt to find happiness I chose to stuff my home with stuff, thinking that trinkets, gadgets and collections could fill a deeper emptiness within me. I started to feel a bit shocked and was showing signs of complex PTSD-Post Traumatic Stress Disorder, however I knew that I needed to "snap out of it" and greet the customers at my garage sale and answer the various questions they had regarding my discarded treasures and momentos. I engaged in the usual and expected bartering and bargaining that is done at garage sales. Sometimes there would be customers that would walk away if they didn't get the price they wanted or they didn't want to pay the extra fifty cents I was asking. Ugh. I told myself that I have to persevere because eventually this garage sale will be over and I will be that much better off physically, mentally and financially.

I sat down with a big sigh and had fleeting thoughts of sadness and began to reminisce about my late mother, Elaine, who also experienced the breakup of her family unit, an unexpected move and most likely had suffered many of the same emotions that I am now experiencing. Of course our situations were different, however I'm sure that after she raised her family and found herself struggling on her own, she experienced a negative change in her finances and ended up having to part with the majority of her possessions in a garage sale. However, I don't think my mom had to endure the complete devastation of finding herself basically penniless, as I did. Don't get me wrong, I was and am so very grateful for the plethora of blessings that I have been given. I know how very fortunate I was to have even lived in such a beautiful home on such a beautiful street in such a beautiful neighborhood and in such a beautiful town. This "American Dream" fantasy, however was abruptly halted by my own choosing. I still felt a deep sense of loss for so many things; not even one neighbor or "friend" that I was close to for 25 years reached out or even now talks with me. Surprisingly, however, I do not feel any anger, regret, sadness, nostalgia or bitterness. I just knew that this was my time to say my premature goodbye to our home and the life I had built. The Beatles said it best, "Money can't buy you love"; that's for sure. Money can actually interfere with the art of mindful living. Goodness in others, such as long-standing neighbors, is not a guarantee. I'll be able to pick up the pieces of my life. I am strong and I am so very capable. I'm thrown back to a record my mom used to listen to when I was growing up: "I Am Woman." The Australian performer Helen Reddy sang it well in her 1970's number-one hit song she co-wrote with Ray Burton: "I am strong. I am invincible. I am woman." In 2014 Helen Reddy was interviewed about this feminist anthem by Houston Public Media and she said that "I Am Woman was delivered from Heaven." I am not surprised that God had his hand in this declaration.

O.K. Getting back to the dragonflies and what happened to me. I was being serenaded by dragonflies, hundreds of them. They were coming from all directions to descend upon and circle me at the cul-de-sac. I was alone, so I was unable to speak to or tell anyone what I was experiencing. I couldn't truly focus on anything except knowing that these dragonflies were all around me and feeling this unbelievable sense of calm. It was magical and surreal. The beauty of the experience was life changing. As I watched all of these dragonflies, I realized and knew without a doubt that they were all there for me. Most definitely. I was their mission, their focus. I had the feeling that I was being engulfed by families and families of all ages and stages. I've now learned that groups of souls tend to reincarnate over and over working out their Karma, their debts owed to others, themselves and the lessons they need to learn. I wondered if these dragonflies were representing people who had lived over the years in what was now our subdivision, but soon realized that would not be the case because the land where my subdivision was erected used to be open land and then a dairy farm. I was reminded of all the encounters with wildlife I experienced over the years I resided in this home. There were the usual neighborhood birds, squirrels and raccoons, but then other unique creatures graced my property. For three years in a row, I witnessed a single crawfish that would emerge from a bubbling hole in the front yard, only to retreat again when he sensed my presence. I happened upon the biggest frog that I've ever seen show up in my garage one rainy day. There were always deer; one year a baby fawn was born right on my front walk. I saw a red fox race through the backyard. There were always nests of eggs to keep tabs on. Mice would get into the house, even though there were snakes around to eat them. One very memorable encounter with the natural world was when I noticed a tiny turtle making its way through my lawn one early morning. I had a sense of wonder and a real connection to living creatures of all kinds. I retraced the path of this tiny turtle to find that it had been newly incubated from one of sixty or so turtle eggs that were grouped under a front yard landscaping boulder and had begun the hatching process. How unusual to find dozens and dozens of little turtles being hatched from eggs that were laid in manicured, suburban landscaping. It was a scene more suitable for the Caribbean when spectators line up with anticipation to witness the turtle hatchlings. I somehow felt it was my job to ensure these turtles' safety and survival. I got a bucket of water and a small sponge to help wipe off the mud from their hatching. I told myself that the turtles were a gift from God. I decided to arrange for a substitute nurse at the hospital that day because it was more important that I stay home and tend to this turtle miracle.

That turtle experience reminded me of a couple of things. One memory was when I was in the 2nd grade and my parents let me stay home from school because I needed to be witness to a unique happening. That morning warranted deviation from the expected schedule and protocol of our established before-school routine. Sometimes it's important to stop and just experience something and take in the wonder. You see, the gym at the college where my dad taught had caught on fire and was burning down. A big building fire was a sight that I had never seen before in my life. This quiet morning was now filled with the sound of sirens from the fire trucks that were racing to the college campus. Our family watched as the firemen were getting set up with their ladders and hoses to battle the blaze. My parents said that my brothers and I should skip school that day to watch the fire and see how the brave firemen (there were no firewomen or firefighters in that era) did their jobs. That experience, and the fact that I was allowed to stay home from school, was very special and always stuck with me. I remember thinking that in the future if I witnessed something big and unique that was happening, I would do the same thing and take an unexpected day off from work. This turtle experience was that day. My "hookie" experience also reminded me of one of my most loved childhood movies, "Chitty Chitty Bang Bang," based on Ian Fleming's novel and adapted for film. There was a scene in the movie where the elite and righteous female lead Truly Scrumptious, artfully portrayed by Sally Ann Howes, confronted Caractacus Pott, portrayed by the infamous Dick Van Dyke, the main character and the dad of two children, Jeremy and Jemima. The issue of concern was that the children were running "wild" in the streets and were not in attendance at school as they should be. The dad's reasoning for their absence was "to give the other children a chance to catch up." That line always stood out to me and was very memorable. We shouldn't always have to follow society's rules and regulations if it means missing out on other real life learning experiences. The Montessori school practices seemed to embrace that philosophy, which was probably a factor in my wanting my children to enroll and participate in Montessori preschool. The dragonflies continued their dance. I would get an occasional dive bomb, almost as if to keep me from fully entering a catatonic state. The dragonflies were waking me up to keep me alert during this amazing spectacle. Time moved so slowly and almost stood still. It's hard to describe the overwhelmingly peaceful feeling that engulfed my being to the core. I felt so much love during this dragonfly serenade. I later read that dragonflies have significant meanings in so many different cultures.

Dragonflies carry with them cultural symbolism that varies from place to place, with most being very positive. People have always been intrigued by this beautiful and magically iridescent and very elegant insect. There are over 5,000 different species of dragonflies or if you are speaking scientifically, Odonata. Even though they are familiar to us in North America, the majority of unique types are found in the remote tropics. Dragonflies are interesting in that they have the ability to move in all directions, 360 degrees, and at a very fast rate of speed. They can also hover while their wings flap around 30 times a second. The Japanese used to call their island Dragonfly Island or Akitsushima. This insect stands for courage and power. In China, dragonflies denote good luck, symbolizing peace, harmony and prosperity. Many Native American cultures believe dragonflies symbolize a rebirth after a very tough time and could be the blessed souls from the dead; that's the version I'm going to gravitate towards as I reflect on my dragonfly and life experience. There is, however, the American folklore where scary dragonflies were used to stitch close the senses (eyes, ears and mouth) of children who misbehave. Dragonflies have been believed to be able to travel between dimensions and are messengers in your dreams. No matter what a particular culture adopts when it comes to the symbolic meaning of dragonflies, in most cultures dragonflies symbolize change, transformation, being able to adapt and come into your own, as in self-actualizing. That is what I'm going through, so it is fitting that I would have dancing dragonflies surround me with love.

Within a minute or so I knew to really try and remember each second because I was aware that this life changing experience would somehow be coming to an end. While I was standing in awe at the cul-de-sac distracted from my original mission of saying goodbye to my beautiful home and what I thought would be my forever life in a pre-mourning of leaving everything behind, I was reminded that I was always humbled and grateful, knowing that I was very lucky to have what I had. Even though I worked very hard to contribute financially and brought home a substantial nursing salary, it turns out that it wasn't enough to keep the lifestyle I was accustomed to having. The hundreds of dragonflies that surrounded me that morning were a wonderful reassurance that I was deeply loved, supported and cared for. I felt that they united themselves to show me that I was not alone. They were there to instill in me the belief that I was going to survive. The dragonflies, which I believe represented generations and generations of loving Spirits, came to support me at my garage sale. As the swarming dragonflies started to dwindle down a bit, I did have the awareness to pull out my iPhone and made the effort to videotape a glimpse of what I was experiencing. I wanted to have some evidence of this dragonfly serenade to replay as proof to myself and others that this experience really did happen and was not a figment of my imagination. I was able to capture the end of the dragonfly dance. A few years after the garage sale, when I was beginning to regain my life and make the transition from surviving to thriving, I found myself strolling into a small diner on a Main Street in Minnesota for a quiet Thanksgiving meal. I didn't realize that this simple road trip would be the extension of the original dragonfly experience I had at my home cul-de-sac during my garage sale.

I went with a close friend for the long Thanksgiving weekend to go downhill skiing at the Wild Mountain Ski Resort in Amador Township, seven miles north of Taylor Falls, Minnesota. It was located in Chisago County, which I remember because the name struck me as odd because it resembled the spelling of the most famous Midwest city, Chicago, and looked like a misprint; even the auto correction on the computer changes the name and thinks it is misspelled. I was just getting back into skiing and this resort actually had snow over the Thanksgiving weekend. I had previously booked a trip out West to ski at Alta in Utah, but just a week before, the Peruvian Resort called with cancellations as there was no snow for any of the runs to be open. Wild Mountain in Minnesota had 26 runs and most of them were available for skiers. I was enjoying the wonder of nature and the simplicity of this rural upper-Midwest town. I strolled Main Street, popping in and out of little "Ma and Pa" shoppes, enjoying viewing the merchandise and handmade crafts and jewelry without the need for purchasing anything. My garage sale experience of parting with so many material things had encouraged me not to feel I had to buy or own the many beautiful things I saw in stores. Empty handed I enjoyed a quiet Thanksgiving dinner at a local diner, trying not to think or wrongly embellish or romanticize the memories of so many previous Thanksgiving celebrations in my past home and life. I had to reinvent myself and start new solo traditions. I felt I was so lucky for making it through this life crisis ordeal. Thank God. In fact, I recently began to pray aloud and literally thank God for my many blessings. That night during my simple and quiet Thanksgiving dinner I thought about my final garage sale and was reminded of the swarm of dragonflies that danced around and dive bombed me. I was again filled with such a beautiful sense of security, love and hope. After dinner, my friend and I decided to take a drive around the snow-covered countryside. I heard that there were a few wineries in these parts, but I was sure that none of them would be open on Thanksgiving night. I still thought it would be fun to venture out and drive around to look for at least one winery, even if I could only view it from afar. We came across a winery by a mistaken wrong turn and to our surprise it was open. As it turns out, this winery prides itself on being open everyday of the year. It was fairly close to the diner we had just enjoyed our Thanksgiving feast at, so it wasn't a long trek or anything. I was still thinking about my dragonfly experience, when I saw the sign, "The Rejoicing Dragonfly Winery." Well, I'll be. Turns out the owner named the winery after a magical experience she had with being surrounded by dragonflies.

In 1995 the owner, who was going through her own personal life change, chose to go on a week-long solo trip where she would canoe the Boundary Waters. She needed to physically and emotionally recover from her losses and reflect about her life. She called it her "walkabout", which is a term used in Australia that philosopher Sam Keene titled a "ménage a moi." The owner was on her final leg of the trip on Horse Lake when a storm came rolling in and she had to take refuge in the only available campsite along the water. The next morning she was greeted by a single dragonfly. Within minutes, however, she was standing among hundreds of dragonflies. They literally danced around her, giving her the most Spiritual encounter of her life. She credits this experience with her following through on her lifelong dream of opening a winery. Naming the winery "The Rejoicing Dragonfly" seemed apropos to honor her metamorphosis and accompanying life changing event. I too, was experiencing a life changing event. It seems that these resulting magical experiences provide us mortals with proof that miracles can and do happen. I hadn't thought about my dragonfly experience since I happened upon the Minnesota winery that healing Thanksgiving. I think, rather, I know that I got a message from Above telling me that what I experienced was in fact really real. Were the dragonflies sent to me from God? Did God lead me to Wild Mountain and Taylor Falls for Thanksgiving so I could come across The Rejoicing Dragonfly Winery? Did a Spirit or Angel prompt me to reflect on my home at the cul-de-sac? Were the dragonflies Spirits or Souls of my departed loved ones? Did God come to my garage sale?

CHAPTER 2

Odetta's Orbs

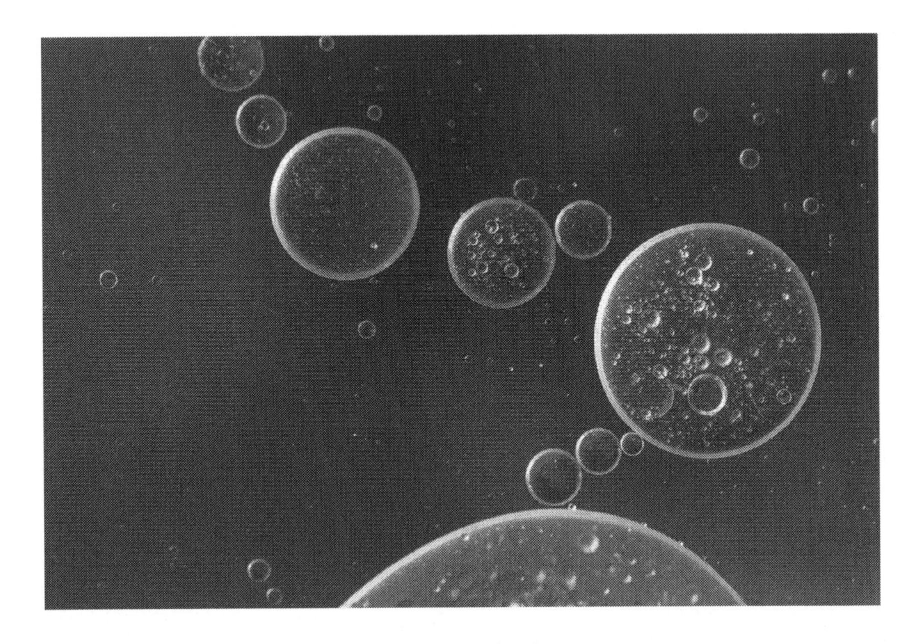

"How great God is! He has given us eyes to see the beauty of the world, hands to touch it, a nose to experience all its fragrance, and a heart to appreciate it all."

Malal Yousafzai

I never knew what an orb was. In fact, I had never even heard of the term. It wasn't until a week after my garage sale when I developed photographs of the remaining garage sale items so I could post them on Offerup, LetGo or Craigslist that I saw these spherical images with very clear faces in them. I had used my old camera, not my phone, and I had put the flash on because it was dusk and I wanted the photographed items to be illuminated. The day after the garage sale was over I brought my camera's flash drive to a photo store and had the clerk print out the photos I took of the leftover stuff so I would have pictures of possible items to sell in the future. It seemed that every photograph was scattered with these various-sized floating and perfectly circular globes. These circles reminded me of the bubble that Glinda The Good Witch from the movie "The Wizard of Oz" came floating down to the earth from out of the Heavens somewhere. In some ways, the orbs also reminded me of when, in the same movie, the Wicked Witch of the West was in the tower and looking through her crystal ball and was able to see Dorothy in real time. At first I thought these circular marks on the photographs were caused from dust in the air or dew drops on the camera lens, however, they seemed too perfectly formed. It appeared there was no way that these sphere-shaped particles were a result of reflection of lights. If it had been raining I could entertain the possibility that what I saw on the developed film and printed photographs were somehow related to moisture, but the weather was perfectly clear for both the days and evenings of the garage sale, so this couldn't be used as a viable explanation or excuse.

I studied the markings of the orbs more closely. The circles actually had a three-dimensional look to them, giving them the appearance of being miniature crystal balls. There were orbs of all shapes and sizes. Their colors were either opaque or semi-transparent. So, if these weren't caused by rain, I went back to the idea that the camera must have picked up some miniscule dust particles in the air. I know that even when the air appears completely clear to the naked eye, it really can contain all sorts of microscopic objects. I remembered when I was a kid and saw this phenomenon first hand. Back in the 1960's people used a slide projector to view personal photographs in which the negatives were very tiny and embedded in these small, thick cardstock square mini-mats. My dad, as a college professor, was very experienced at using slides and slide projectors in his classes and would often bring the machine home so that our family could view our photos from our many travels, especially our year long family trip to Greece. We also viewed photos of birthdays and holiday events using the slide projector. I remember the slides were painstakingly and carefully pre-loaded into this circular carousel and a button would be pushed to advance to the next image. We would put a sheet up on the wall and attach it to the fake wood paneling (the hip decor of that decade) which would serve as a makeshift screen. When the lights were turned off and we would be able to see the images on the slides, the path that the projector light would take would show loads and loads of dust particles just moving about in the air.

I showed the garage sale photos from that night to my friend Odetta. She said that the circular and spherical globe images at my garage sale were orbs and that I was surrounded by Spirits. She went on to say that these globe-like bubbles on my photos were actually my deceased loved ones, ancestors, animals and other Spirits. She instructed me to look closely and focus on the inside of the orbs. Many of them were extremely small, but no matter what the size, it was clear that there were faces in each orb. Some were of people and some were of animals. Odetta said that this was proof that there was some higher power entity among us, and around me specifically as I was going through this challenging and transformational personal time in my life. She pointed out the orbs in the garage, on the driveway and near the house. She assured me that there was nothing to worry about and that I was being watched over and blessed with positive and protective energy. What I saw in the photographs was mind-blowing! I later called up Odetta to speak with her again about the orbs and asked her how she first learned about orbs. She said she had attended an Indianapolis IANDS-International Association for Near Death Studies presentation back in 2012 where a presenter showed slides and discussed the orb phenomenon. She then tried to capture orbs on her own using her simple digital flash camera. Odetta found that her camera (and that of two different friends' cameras to make sure what she was seeing was actually there and not just a result of her particular device) could photograph these unique circles and spheres whether she was inside the house, outside in the yard at dusk or when the skies were darker in the evening. It just seemed that a flash was needed. Odetta's orbs were concentrated around trees, bushes and grasses with many of the orbs suspended in the air. There were also orbs surrounding humans and animals. Odetta wondered if the orbs were stationary, so she conducted her own novice experiment to find the answer to this question. She would take a series of 15-20 photos in the same place, utilizing a tripod to make sure there was little variance or accidental movement. When she did this and she developed the film, she confirmed that these orbs do in fact move. Certain orbs even followed her dogs when they moved from one end of the room to another. After closer examination, Odetta saw that the facial features located inside of the orbs were quite realistic and many were recognizable. Odetta was a dog breeder and knew the unique facial features of most every dog in her care. She said that when looking at the orbs she could actually identify certain breeds she worked with due to their coloring and unique facial features. She also said she saw her grandmother, along with many other faces she could not recognize, including a Native American Indian Chief.

Selling most of my belongings at my garage sale was an emotionally-charged, yet very necessary endeavor. There were times I felt very all alone. The reality that life as I knew it was coming to a crossroads left me gasping for air. I looked around at my garage sale wares and became disgusted with the excessive remnants of some illusion that I had been creating and living in. No wonder why there is a societal trend for less consumerism and materialism. People are now building and moving into customized "tiny houses" and living as minimalists off grid. I get it now, but I sure didn't all those years when I was building what I thought would be the perfect life. I was drowning in a sea of accumulated stuff. My emotions ran high and included feeling embarrassed that our family had collected so much in the way of material belongings. I took ownership in all of this and felt shame and guilt. I grew accustomed to the excess. I looked around at the stuff set out for the garage sale and I saw numerous now unwanted items that represented my life. This was just what could be seen on the outside, on the driveway. Inside my soul I was dealing with the aftermath and sadness of the deterioration of life as I knew it.

I never was much into buying things until I owned my first home. I prided myself in being a homemade kind of girl, making do with what I had and creating from scratch and everyday items or objects easily found in nature. I think I eventually purchased things to fill the emptiness I felt inside. I was responsible for doing all of the shopping for the home and family, whether it was the groceries, furniture, toiletries or home repair items, so regular trips to the store were necessary. Now I needed to declutter and part with so much stuff. It was a loss on many levels. My mother used to say to me that I was one of God's favorite pupils because I always had to learn lessons the hard way. Now that I was alone in this big house and trying to get rid of as much as I could, I was somewhat comforted by this orb possibility. What if there really were orbs everywhere, floating around us mortals as we go about our lives? If that were so, then I shouldn't feel alone and I should feel that I have support from the Spirit world. Maybe God was really at my garage sale; I surely had a great number of indications that I was in the midst of an Awakening. I was hoping that I was surrounded by any good and positive entity, as I was having to sell practically all of my belongings which resulted in me feeling a great deal of sadness, disbelief and fear for what my future might hold. This thought about fear reminded me of late and great Nelson Mandela, the South African anti-apartheid revolutionary and philanthropist president (actually the country's first black head of state and first elected representative in the democratic election) who discussed fear and that people who are fearless actually have to work on triumphing over it. He was best known for spending and surviving 27 years in prison, eventually being awarded the Nobel Peace Prize along with South African President F. W. De Klerk for their efforts to rid the country of the apartheid system. Mandela is now known to the latest generation as being an inspirational Civil Rights activist. In 2009 in honor of Mandela's birthday, July 18th was declared Mandela Day to acknowledge and promote global peace and celebrate his accomplishments.

I always loved watching movies with a message. Some of my go-to movies were: "Rudy", "Stand and Deliver", "The Pursuit of Happyness", "The Blind Side", "Lean On Me", "Freedom Writers", "Good Will Hunting", "Forrest Gump", "Dead Poet's Society", "The Great Debaters", "Hoosiers" and "Coach Carter." "Coach Carter" was one of my favorites. It is an American biographical sports drama about a basketball coach who became well-known for suspending his undefeated team because they didn't make the grade, academically speaking. I remember feeling chills go down my spine when in the movie, one of the students stood up and recited a quote from memory that I thought was from Nelson Mandela because Mandela read parts of it in his inauguration speech, but was in fact written by self-help guru Marianne Williamson from her 1989 Spiritual best-selling book A Return To Love. It went like this: "Our deepest fear is not that we are weak. Our deepest fear is that we are powerful beyond measure. It is our light, not our darkness that most frightens us. We ask ourselves, who am I to be brilliant, gorgeous, talented, fabulous? Actually, who are you not to be? You are a child of God. Your playing small does not serve the world. There is nothing enlightened about shrinking so that other people won't feel insecure around you. We are all meant to shine as children do. It's not just in some of us; it is in everyone. And as we let our own light shine, we unconsciously give other people permission to do the same. As we are liberated from our own fear, our presence automatically liberates others."

I wonder if people through the existence of time on earth saw orbs but had a fear of them. There is documentation of spherical objects called orbs in John Mitton's 1890 poem known as "The Ptolemaic." He states that the earth is at the center of a series of orbs or spheres of space. He questioned whether this phenomenon was attributed to more Angelic forces "with Centric and Eccentric scribbled o'er, Cycle and Epicycles, Orb in Orb" rather than to celestial science. The 18th century, which marked a time when technology and documentation was advancing because of the invention of the printing press, writers' poems (some about orbs) were able to be distributed so people could read about and contemplate others' observations and experiences in printed manuscripts. One book contained "The semi-globes or electrical orbs. A poem." Planets and the sun were called orbs. It wasn't until scientist and neurosurgeon Dr. Norman Shelley, M.D., Ph. D. had his own mystical experience and chose to freely write about it that people started to make a Spiritual connection with orbs. He wrote, "Orbs may be to the atmosphere what crop circles are to the earth. Having seen orbs and had them photographed while I was speaking, it is great to know that we are receiving cosmic energetic communication." Krause Heinemann who holds a Ph.D. in Experimental Physics for NASA wrote, "There is no doubt in my mind that the orbs may well be one of the most significant 'outside of this reality' phenomena mankind has ever witnessed" after he and his wife conducted numerous experiments with orbs to rule out any doubt. He believed he witnessed some form of paranormal intelligence.

Nowadays there are extensive amounts of anecdotal and scientific evidence that the Spirit world exists, yet acceptance of such is still in the early stages. Sedona, Arizona held the world's first conference on orbs where numerous scientific professionals confirmed their existence. Physicist and professor William Tiller, who spent 35 years researching consciousness and matter at Stanford University in California, stated that our eyes can only see ten percent of the known universe, yet we know other phenomena exists. Documented proof of orbs has been found in photographs all over the world. Michael Ledwith, professor at the National University of Ireland and a member of the International Theological Commission at the Vatican in Italy, has a collection of over 100,000 orb pictures ranging in shapes, sizes and colors. Many of these images have faces within them, possibly of Spirits of those who have passed on or those waiting to be born into a physical body. Currently, there are many essays and reports written on orbs, however their widespread acceptance is in the infancy stage.

If orbs were surrounding me and all of us, then without my knowing, I was supported by great love. If only there were undeniable proof. Well, proof that I could actually see came as my garage sale photographs were developed and I saw orbs with my own eyes. I remember taking an art history class and seeing orb-like depictions where people had halos over them; so many of the religious paintings of people donn halos. These orbs were described by my friend Odetta as slices of moments in time that reveal to our eyes that there are indeed other forms of consciousness that are present in this earthly realm. These glimpses into the other side seem to be only visible by the flashes of light produced by a camera. These flashes seem to pierce the veil between Heaven and earth. Who and what are they? Are they our deceased loved ones? Maybe. So many accounts of witnesses to this orb phenomenon state that they do not know even though many of the faces are recognizable. The shear numbers of orbs that grace our presence may mean that these are a collective of the many, if not all, Spirits that were once part of our world. They are us, or at least they were us at one point. These entities surround us without us even being aware that they are there. They were most definitely there as I was forced into unloading the excess of earthly belongings from my dream home. I saw them in photos I later developed. Did these orbs surround me with love? Was Odetta's knowledge of orbs coincidental? Did God come to my garage sale?

CHAPTER 3

Gerard - The Patron Saint of Mothers and The Yellow Corvette

"God's dream is that you and I and all of us will realize that we are family, that we are made for togetherness, for goodness, and for compassion."

Desmond Tutu

Gerard was my grade school neighbor Steve's middle name. In fact, his five siblings also shared that same middle name. I asked him if Gerard was a family name that was passed down; I assumed it was because many middle names are family names that go back numerous generations. Steve told me that his mom had trouble conceiving and with each pregnancy attempt, as a devout Catholic, she would pray to the Patron Saint of Mothers, Saint Gerard Magella. As Catholics, Steve's family prescribed to the accepted traditional ideology and rituals associated with their religion. His mother's prayers were always answered and she was blessed with six healthy and beautiful children. I never gave this another thought until I was ready to start my own family and found myself having some difficulty getting pregnant. I had no idea that years later I would revisit the life-altering significance and affirmation of praying to Saint Gerard, let alone God's power. It really confirms for me that there are reasons and meanings for every event that transpires and there are Spiritual lessons embedded deep into our life experiences.

I was busy getting ready for the big garage sale. As I opened up my four-car garage to start moving out the folding tables and setting up, a yellow corvette pulled up to my driveway and slowed to a halt for what I thought was for the driver to peruse my wares. The windows were tinted so I couldn't get a clear view of the driver or passenger; they seemed to stay there for an unusually long time. In fact, they stayed so long that I was tempted to go up to the car and see if they wanted anything, but I was busy and didn't want to take the time. The yellow corvette surely got my attention though. I was then almost instantaneously teleported back to an experience I had twenty years before which happened just a couple of blocks away from my house. It was like I was daydreaming, but I remember I actually felt like I was physically reliving this event in the past that I had only thought about a few times over the many years and never really gave any significance to. Many, many years ago one morning I made the decision to drive to the grocery store a couple of blocks away from home to get some cream for my coffee. I consider myself to be a "dairy girl" and have grown accustomed to including organic, pasture-raised half-and-half cream in my morning coffee; nowadays I only consume A2 milk because it contains the healthier milk protein casein. Midway to the store and as I was turning right on the side road for the back entrance of the store, I was cut off by a speeding yellow corvette whose driver failed to yield. If it wasn't for my quick reflexes to slam on the breaks, the result may have ended in a major collision. Even though the sports car was speeding, I remember focusing on the license plate as time seemed to go in slow motion. I could see that the license plate read "GERARD." This really got my attention, so much so that I drove back home forgetting the reason I was in the car and on the way to the store in the first place.

I longed for a child. There were three kids in my family growing up and I always pictured myself with kids. Over the years I've heard a number of friends and neighbors share with me their infertility challenges. I had some difficulty conceiving, but nothing near like some of the horror and heartbreaking stories I had heard. I can vividly remember sitting in my 6th grade Health class during Sex Education at my middle school watching "The Movie" where all of the female students (the boys and girls from gym class were segregated in those days; there was no coed) were taught about "the birds and the bees." Back then, many parents didn't even bother giving "The Talk" because they knew their children would be told "The Facts of Life" in school. I can't remember much from the presentation, because I think it was more movie than discussion, but the take-away for me was that it only takes one time of "going all the way" for girls to become pregnant. My "biological clock was ticking" as Marisa Tomei famously said in the 1992 movie "My Cousin Vinny." This biological clock for me was all-consuming, weighing heavy on my heart, clouding my everyday thoughts and actions. It took over my common sense and long-range outlook. My desire for having a child became my sole focus; I always knew that my greatest goal and accomplishment in life would be motherhood. My best friend reminded me of how obsessed I was when it came to my wanting to get pregnant. She witnessed many months come and go where I was left in tears because the pregnancy test indicators showed minus signs instead of plus signs. One evening my best friend came over to find me uncontrollably crying. She assumed it was because I confirmed again that I wasn't pregnant. As it turned out, my being beyond distraught was actually because the new striped sheets that I purchased and were expecting to be delivered that day were backordered. Yep, I was inconsolable because I would have to wait another two weeks for my new sheets. Pretty dramatic, as backordered sheets did not warrant such an extreme emotional reaction. I knew then that I needed some sort of new strategy to conceive. I thought I had exhausted everything I could do except look into fertility, and that is when I thought I should pray. Why I didn't think of this first was because I considered myself an Atheist and didn't put much value in prayer. Then I remembered that my childhood neighbor Steve's mom had experienced trouble conceiving and she prayed to the Patron Saint Gerard Majella. After that, miracles happened for her and she was able to get pregnant. She was blessed with six children and because she believed that Patron Saint Gerard was responsible for her pregnancy miracles, she made sure each of her six children's middle names were Gerard. I decided to give prayer a try. I waited until I had the house to myself and didn't have any distractions. It was a Sunday morning. My mind was calm and clear, so it was a perfect time to focus on prayer. The words that I spoke when I prayed were very simple and went like this: "Dear Patron Saint Gerard, I understand that you are the Patron Saint of Mothers and were instrumental in helping a mom I know conceive her six children. I am asking you to please help me and bless me. I want to get pregnant more than anything. I will be forever grateful and appreciative. Thank you Patron Saint Gerard. Janet."

It was that very same day that I had a mystical experience with the yellow corvette and the Gerard license plate. The next day I found out I was pregnant! I believe that Saint Gerard answered my prayer. You see, what happened was that I decided to run back out to the store, this time not for cream, but to pick up another pregnancy test; this was almost getting to be a weekly ritual. I pulled out of the subdivision and turned right onto a side road, which was a shortcut to the store. There was no traffic; the road was empty. What happened next would be one of the events that changed my beliefs forever, as it was one of many STEs-Spiritually Transformative Encounters I had experienced. Little did I know that twenty years later at my garage sale I would be reminded of what happened back then, which turned out to be the start of my Spiritual Awakening. Out of literally nowhere, on this desolate back road, a sporty, bright yellow corvette sharply turned in front of me failing to yield as it was turning left. I slammed on my brakes to avoid a collision, but I knew to look at the license plate so I could possibly report this erratic and reckless driver. I thought I would have a hard time remembering the letters and/or numbers of the license plate, but I had to give it a try. To my amazement, everything seemed to go in slow motion at that point. I was able to specifically see the license plate as the car almost seemed to stop right in front of me. It was a vanity plate that was clearly labeled GERARD. This experience happened just prior to me going out when I was making a concerted effort to pray to the Patron Saint Gerard Majella, asking him to intervene in my overwhelming desire to get pregnant. Wow! What were the odds that I would see a license plate with this name? I didn't just see it, I experienced it as time went into slow motion after I was cut off by the yellow corvette that came out of nowhere on an empty road. I still wanted to report the driver because this situation could have ended in a tragic accident, but the moment that thought came to my mind, the yellow corvette completely disappeared from the area and all I thought about was the name Gerard. So, the car was speeding, then almost stopped at a standstill one moment and then vanished the next. It seemed odd to me. I thought it was a mystery, but I didn't analyze it too much. I mentioned the situation to a few people, but nobody really seemed to care or think anything was unusual. I went back home forgetting why I ventured out in the first place. Later on that day it dawned on me that I never picked up that pregnancy test, so I went back to the store to pick up one. I had to wait until the morning to do the test because it requires that you use the first morning's urine. I had already spent a small fortune on these tests, but I was determined to keep trying and keep testing. To my absolute and utter delight, the next morning's test was positive! I was pregnant! I sometimes credited that my getting pregnant had to do with praying to Saint Gerard, but for the most part I didn't think too much about that and went on with my life. Every now and then I would share the story of the amazing coincidence that took place that morning, where I prayed to Saint Gerard and then saw the name Gerard on the license plate of the yellow corvette that cut me off, just to find out that I was pregnant the very next day. Nine months later I gave birth to my first child and my dream of being a mother became a reality.

Here I sit at my garage sale twenty years later, amazed that I just saw a yellow corvette and that it paused in front of my driveway long enough for me to take notice and be reminded of my Saint Gerard experience a couple of decades earlier. I had no idea this garage sale weekend would bring numerous other Spiritual experiences that would collectively cause a major shift in my belief system. I think about my children and what a blessing they have been in my life. My gaze turned to the stuff I am selling. In a way, the process of gathering, sorting, pricing, selling and discarding the remnants of my old life give me some hope that in the future I will be more streamlined and I'll be more discerning about what items I choose to acquire. I had always been the one who handled most everything in the home. I worked full-time as a nurse, taught evening ESL-English as a Second Language classes two days a week at the local library and volunteered with numerous events. I was used to multitasking and doing a lot on my own. To save money I picked up unique treasures from secondhand shops to help create the look and environment of a classy, suburban home. I was proud of the useful and beautiful items that I acquired that contributed to creating a very comfortable and gorgeous living space. I took on this responsibility joyfully and willingly. I found myself shopping the local resale shops, Goodwill and Savers acquiring items that were worth a great deal more than their price tag. I guess over the years the items accumulated. As a result, I certainly had a lot to discard at the garage sale.

My work as a nurse, volunteering and managing my family and home fulfilled me. Now I'm brought back here to the garage sale, where I'm saying "goodbye" to the possessions and remnants of my bittersweet life. My thoughts return to my children and home. I'm flooded with the feeling of being blessed even though my current financial outcome and situation is not ideal and certainly not how I envisioned my life. I am forever grateful to the Patron Saint Gerard Majella for answering my prayers and blessing me. As I watched the yellow corvette pull away from my cul-de-sac, I asked myself so many questions. Was it a coincidence that I remembered my grade school neighbor Steve's mom's prayers to Saint Gerard that led her to assigning the name Gerard to all six of her children's middle names? Did my own prayers to Saint Gerard have a hand in my getting pregnant? Was the yellow corvette the same car from twenty years prior? Did Spirit coordinate the name on the license plate? Did God come to my garage sale?

CHAPTER 4

The Italian-Charmed Bangled Biker Gal

"The day science begins to study non-physical phenomena, it will make more progress in one decade than in all the previous centuries of its existence. To understand the true nature of the universe, one must think in terms of energy, frequency and vibration."

Nikola Tesla

The crowds flocked to her as if she was the Messiah. These garage sale shoppers seemed to be in a trance as they left their perusing one by one and headed down to the end of the driveway towards my mailbox where this woman held court. I've seen this type of collective mass movement toward someone years back when the discount department store chain K-Mart had their limited-in-time "Blue Light Specials." She was next to my mailbox, which was just off the main street of my cul-de-sac. She must have been standing on a boulder or crate or box of some sort because she was a good two-feet above the dozen or so people who were gathered around her. I didn't notice it at the time, but after she left I saw that there was no boulder, crate or box that she could have been standing on left behind. The scene was unbelievable and something that you would not see at a garage sale. It reminded me of when I saw street performers in downtown Indianapolis in what the city folk call "busking," promoted by the Arts Council of Indianapolis, Indianapolis Downtown, Inc. and the arts group IndyFringe. While it was happening I just observed in amazement, and when it was over I was awestruck. Was this lady a real person or an Angel or Jesus or God? She had to have risen up high on her own, as there was no evidence that could otherwise explain how she got above the crowd that was gathered below. I remember thinking how strange it was that this woman pulled up to my house, saw my bike for sale and asked me to hold it for an hour while she got some money. Yet, even though she walked back down to the end of the driveway, I thought to go get money, she never even left my property. She didn't get in her car to drive off to the nearest ATM or grocery store to get cash to pay for the bike. Instead, within minutes she was surrounded by people who were attentively listening to whatever she was saying. When I saw the number of people at the mailbox, twelve to be exact, like Christ's twelve Disciples or Apostles, I thought that was odd because I didn't even remember more than one or two people at the garage sale at that time. Where did all these people come from and how did they get there so fast without my seeing them drive or walk up? I continued to sit in my folding chair sheltered by the shade from being inside my garage. You would think that I would have walked down to the mailbox to see firsthand what this was all about, but I didn't. That thought didn't even cross my mind. A neighbor named John stopped by to ask how my garage sale was going. I replied, "good." My focus turned away from the lady who wanted to buy my bike and was now involved in some mystical experience at my mailbox. I didn't say anything to John about how odd it was and he didn't say anything about it to me either.

I had gone through a three-month period where I was somewhat obsessed with buying these small, often personalized little metal rectangle jewelry pieces that connected to one another very neatly to create bracelets. These were called Italian Charms and they were all the rage, perfect for someone like me that really liked more meaningful, personalized jewelry. I had no intention of selling these, but I brought them out so I could work on connecting them to keep me busy when the garage sale traffic was slower. John, my neighbor, commented on how many charms I had and how expensive they all must have been. I told him that many of them were under a dollar. Actually some of them were under fifty cents, which made them so affordable that you could start a huge collection of them and not think you would be spending much. I guess this contributed to my justification for going crazy buying and collecting these charms. I never owned a traditional charm bracelet as a kid like many of my friends did, so I gave my adult self permission to start a charm bracelet. These Italian charms were very easy and convenient to order online. I found that on eBay you could get these Italian Charms personalized, so I was adding five, sometimes ten more charms to my collection. I felt I was not only getting a deal, but I was getting a steal. I knew I had more charms than the average person should have had. I felt a tinge of guilt that my collection, which started out innocently enough, turned into more. At least my obsession was somewhat short-lived as I did have a stopping point of a couple of months to the purchasing. The reality of the situation was that my at times excessive tendencies, as evidenced by my needing to have yet another garage sale to purge the stuff that was replaced by the new stuff, definitely had a role in my starting and adding to the Italian Charm collection. I was reminded of my brother Wade's rendition of the late American stand-up observational and sarcastic comedian George Carlin's monologue about people and their stuff and needing to find new places for their stuff. Carlin joked that having stuff contributes to adding meaning to our lives and that is one of the main reasons why we have houses. "Houses are places to keep your stuff when you're out looking for more stuff," he would say. Our family's accumulated stuff turned out to be a burden that would occupy a great deal of my time as I had to deal with the decisions of sorting out what stuff to use, keep or discard. It is embarrassing to admit, but when all was said and done, I had enough small Italian Charms to construct three very generous-sized belts. O.K. I came clean. I don't believe I reached "hoarder" status, but I came close to the realization that I was filling the empty spaces in my life with stuff. As I embark on my solo healing journey, I now understand the reason for and can justify this overindulgence. I loved things personalized, still do; personalized items seem to have so much more meaning. Other people must think so too, because even to this day you can find name key chains at the local gas stations or car washes or novelty stores including Target and 5-Below. I've always been drawn to those display racks that list various names in alphabetical order. There was also a phase where some of the mid-range jewelry stores would carry these round, glass lockets that you can place various mini-trinkets in to personalize the necklace, bracelet or pin in a more adult way than a brightly colored kid-like keychain. I've acquired those too and filled them with personalized trinkets. Some people add scissors if they are a hairdresser, or a cross if they are religious, or a military emblem for their service, or a musical note if they play an instrument, or a horse if they are an equestrian, etc. You get the picture. The next big trend, the one that eventually led me to a pretty Spiritual experience with regards to this gal that wanted to buy my bike from the garage sale and ended up being surrounded by a crowd, was my Italian charm collection. The Italian Charm trend spread like wildfire across the nation. My first purchases were personalized charms with family names. Then I added birthstones of my children and their hobbies. I went on to add charms that represented my interests and my job as a nurse. Then there seemed to be a need to add symbols of the places I had travelled to. The opportunities to find charm options were endless. So, you can see how this really could get out of control. Most people would have kept it simple and exercised some constraint, but not me. I felt some satisfaction in finding and acquiring these charms. It felt almost therapeutic until I had to change my life focus from accumulating to decluttering. I was now forced to sell any excess possessions. Somehow, though, I couldn't part with the Italian Charm collection; at least they didn't take up much room. They had served some purpose. Maybe focusing on the charms brought me happiness and was the distraction I needed at the time.

So this lady wanted to buy my bike. I was saving it for her while she supposedly was going to run to the closest ATM or store to get cash, yet she never made it past my mailbox. People flocked to her from nowhere, and there she was suspended in the air talking, almost preaching, to exactly twelve people. It was a crazy and unbelievable scene, yet at the same time I wasn't phased enough to go check it out or react in any way. When I looked at her, both of her outstretched arms were covered from her wrists to her elbows with bracelets all made from Italian Charms. This surely got my attention as I was just thinking about and talking about my excessive amounts and collection of Italian Charms. I thought to myself that this was such a coincidence. I was thinking about Italian Charms and then here was this lady, who I started to call the biker gal, with more Italian Charms than I had ever seen in one place, except for my collection of course. The biker gal captivated the crowd with her Italian Charmed bangles covering both of her arms, which were spread out like she was blessing her followers. With my interest in and analyzing of how special each and every charm was, even in my excess, you would think that I would go over to this lady, not just to see her bracelets and ask her about the meaning of each of her charms (because I know that each charm held a significance), but just to check out what was going on. These people at her feet were mesmerized. Where did they all come from? I don't even remember anyone even being at my garage sale when she drove up. I figured at some point she would come up to me to pay for the bike, so I really wasn't feeling any strong need to approach her. Anyway, by the look of what was going on there with this bangled, biker gal, there were more important things happening by the mailbox and I really didn't want to interfere. Also, I felt I was in a slow motion trance.

I turned my gaze away from the preaching scene because a man came up to me wanting to pay for his chosen garage sale items of a couple of Indiana Pacers sweatshirts and a puzzle. The transaction was swift and simple. After I bagged up his treasures, I turned back to check out was was happening with the bangled, biker gal. To my amazement she was gone, along with the large group that had surrounded her at the mailbox for what seemed to be at least an hour. Where did she go? Where did all those people go? How could they all have been there for so long and then gone instantly when I turned away for just a few minutes while I tended to one customer? I began to question whether or not I had imagined the entire situation or if it had really happened. It couldn't have been in my mind. I clearly remember the lady coming up to me and wanting to buy my bike, but not having any money with her. I remember seeing the crowd around her. I vividly remember seeing that her body was slightly raised in the air at the mailbox and thinking about how odd that sight was. I remember seeing that both of her arms were covered with rows and rows of Italian-Charmed bracelets. I looked at the bike she had wanted. It was still parked outside of my garage on hold and moved aside away from the rest of the items for sale. Should I put the bike back out? Something told me to leave it and that this lady would return to follow through with her purchase. Sure enough, she returned. She didn't say much about anything and made no mention to talking with that crowd of people. For some reason, I didn't even think to ask her about it, even though I really had a great many questions I could have asked. Something prevented me from even thinking to engage in a conversation with her, as if I was in shock or something. She reached out to hand me the money for the bike. I was selling the bike for $45, and she handed me a $100 bill. I reached in my fanny pack to get her change, but she told me to keep the change. I told her I couldn't keep the change as the change was more than the bike itself. She said that she knows how people never get what they should when they sell things at garage sales and insisted that I keep the difference. I reluctantly accepted it. The entire transaction and conversation was done in what felt like slow motion. I felt time warped and I was moving through thick, clear jello. I remember her thanking me for holding the bike for her and trusting that she would return to pay for it. I thanked her for her kindness and generosity. I glanced at her arms, remembering that when I saw her before they were covered with numerous bracelets made from Italian Charms. However, her arms were bare, except for a watch she wore on her left wrist. O.K. That's weird. I know what I saw before. I wanted to ask her about her bracelets, but she began walking away with the bike.

I remember seeing the wheels of the bike moving as she was leaving down the driveway, but for some reason I didn't see her legs or feet touching the ground. It looked like she was walking the bike to her car, but she wasn't walking. She seemed to be floating away while she was guiding the bike down the driveway. I just stood and stared in disbelief. Just like some of the other mystical situations I experienced at my garage sale, time just seemed to go in slow motion. I didn't think to talk to anyone about it or even go towards her to check it out. It was if my energy was drained and my body, including my arms, legs and mouth just couldn't move. I could see very clearly though. I don't have any recollection of her putting the bike into a car and driving away; she may have, but I just can't remember. I knew I needed to sit down to take this all in. I saw my Italian Charm belt collection and thought it was so strange that this lady who bought my bike had excessive amounts of these charms at one point and then they were gone. I know that the Italian-Charmed biker gal came to my garage sale, but was she a person or an Angel or some kind of preacher because of the crowd of twelve people gathered around her as she was elevated into the air? Were these Italian charms mystical momentos? Did I imagine this almost religious scene at my mailbox? Did God come to my garage sale?

CHAPTER 5

Psychics, Mediums, Near Death Experiences and IANDS

"God grant me the serenity to accept the things I cannot change, the courage to change the things I can, and the wisdom to know the difference."

Reinhold Niebuhr

I grew up with the absence of any significant exposure to organized religion. Plus, I never even really had an interest in learning about it. I guess, then, I would call myself an Atheist. My father, a history professor emeritus from a small, liberal arts college in Indiana, who had great knowledge of and respect for the world's various religions, was a self-proclaimed devout Atheist. I really don't remember discussing religion with my mom, but I was aware that she grew up Catholic. I remember when I was a child around six or seven years old I did spend part of a day at a Quaker church in a nearby town. It was called the Friends Meeting House and I was not supposed to use the word "church" because there was no steeple. I recall just sitting in this circular pew seating area where I wasn't allowed to say a word and nobody could talk with me. The worship space was extremely simple with the absence of any religious or liturgical symbols. The windows were super high so you couldn't look outside. Looking back as an adult I really think that maybe my Quaker experience was because my parents needed some kind of childcare for me for the day, because I don't remember either of my parents staying there with me and I never returned there again. I had only a couple of other religious experiences growing up. Another church experience was when I was ten years old and our family moved to Acharnes, a suburb of Athens, Greece, when my dad founded and began the first ever Athens history study abroad program at his college in the early 1970's. Our entire family relocated there for a year and stayed on afterwards as my Atheist dad finished writing a book, a book on religion! My experience in Greece was absolutely amazing. When I was sitting at my garage sale I got into a conversation with a Greek family who suggested that I donate any garage sale leftovers to Holy Trinity Greek Orthodox Cathedral as they were having a rummage sale the following weekend, so I decided to share with them my experience of being exposed to the Greek Orthodox Church. We got into a very deep and long discussion about organized religion and the existence of God. My brothers Harold and Wade and I attended the local Greek school, as my parents believed in full-immersion when it came to cultures, languages and kids attending elementary schools in foreign countries. It was customary for all school children to attend church on Saturdays, so unlike the United States where kids go to school Monday through Friday, in Greece, grade school was six days. When in Greece, do as the Greeks, and so I attended school on Saturdays. Saturdays were devoted to studying the Greek Orthodox religion and attending church. The Greek orthodox church is one of the autocephalous churches that build upon the orthodox Christianity founded by Saint Paul. After singing the Greek national anthem and participating in our lessons, the entire school of students Kindergarten through 6th grade (around 150 kids) along with the teachers (one per grade) and the headmaster would walk approximately one mile on the dirt road to the Greek Orthodox Church, The Coptic Orthodox Church of St. Mary and St. Mark, which was on the other side of town. I distinctly remember the odor that permeated the sacred space (now I am aware that the church officials were burning frankincense) and receiving ribbons with various religious medallions every week.

Oh yeah, there was one other religious experience that stands out in my mind. My best childhood friend and neighbor Maria snuck me into her church service one day when we were about twelve years old. Her family members were devout Catholics and usually went to church every Sunday. They would attend St. Malachy Catholic Church in Brownsburg, but occasionally they would go to a service put on at the local Catholic grade school. On this particular Sunday, Maria was instructed by her parents to attend the St. Malachy Catholic mass by herself, as they had to visit her grandparents. So, on the way, Maria came by my house and asked if I wanted to go with her. She didn't explain much about what I would expect; she just said for me to put on a dress and just follow her and whenever I would see her do something like stand or kneel or walk up to the altar, just to imitate her and do the same. So I went. The experience seemed so weird as it was not that interactive and it was almost robotic. After the service Maria showed me something that she and her brothers and sisters would do if they got the chance and wouldn't be caught. She took me through the building and we went up to the fourth floor and through a secret door. When she opened the door we were at the top of a spiral fire escape that looked like one of those slides from an indoor water park. It was made of metal and Maria said that as you slide down your butt would stick to the surface if it was hot and you had shorts on. Maria happened to bring two pillowcases which she had folded up and stuffed in her pockets. We used them to slide down the spiral slide with ease and speed. It was so much fun we did it five more times. The sixth time a nun yelled at us and threw cold water down the slide in an attempt to punish us or at least shoo us away so we would be deterred from a repeat future ride. It didn't work, as trespassing and riding the spiral fire escape slide became a tradition we continued until the religious school closed its doors when we were in high school.

My parents told me that they didn't believe there was a God, but that I could believe whatever I wanted to. They said that, yet they didn't expose me to the options. They compared people to all things living, like a plant, and that people had a birth and a death and that was that. Nothing more. I always had a nagging feeling that there had to be more. My feeling eventually led me to attend, join and even be baptized in the Presbyterian Church when I was in college, and then later I converted to Catholicism. I "religiously" practiced religion in a church, even becoming a lector for a decade, but did so without really researching it or looking into the Spiritual aspects of the stories in the Bible. I got to talking to a customer at my garage sale. She introduced herself as Dana. We started a pretty superficial conversation. I knew she was making an effort to reach out to me, but I wasn't really reciprocating by contributing much or sharing with her. I wasn't even providing the non-verbal gestures and intermittent reinforcement that people do in casual encounters that would encourage a person to continue their efforts to communicate and reach out, yet this Dana lady kept talking with me. Dana went on to say that going to garage sales and looking at other's earthly and once-loved belongings has been a sort of therapy for her. She continued to talk and say that "garage saling" has given her a sense of community without having to join a support group or pay for costly counseling sessions. Now this was getting more personal. In her case, as she appeared to be a rather reserved and soft-spoken woman, she definitely seemed to step out of her comfort zone to even strike up a conversation with me. The conversation was fairly one-sided on her end. I continued to be somewhat disinterested. I don't even remember talking with her that long. After taking a look at the plethora of household goods for sale and then taking a look at me, she said that she knew exactly what I was going through. She shared that not long before, she had to sell most of her belongings and leave her life and home. She recounted how shocked and surprised she was that her monetary security, comfort and cherished belongings were really an illusion after she was forced to face the reality of her situation. I didn't feel the need or even had the energy to confirm her comments or add anything personal. I just smiled and thanked her for sharing. I'm not quite sure how our conversation turned to the topic of the universe and its vast deepness, but it did. This garage sale customer, Dana, may or may not have known that she was about to change my life forever with her next suggestion. She said I should consider opening up my worldview and explore what she believed was the reality of life after death. Really? How did the conversation turn to this? In fact, it seemed that her mission in coming to my garage sale was not to buy anything, but to relay this message to expand my thinking and then give me a specific direction that would help open my heart and mind.

Dana told me that she attends monthly IANDS-International Association for Near-Death Studies meetings at Butler University's Edison-Duckwall Recital Hall in Indianapolis. She sat and talked with me for over an hour about the various speakers that would either present their NDEs or would perform readings because they were self-acclaimed psychic mediums. She said that the speakers and attendees at these monthly meetings, sharing their first-hand accounts and evidence of life after death, have not only helped her to emotionally heal, but have opened up an entire new world of Spiritual thought for her. She said that IANDS and some readings she has had with psychic mediums have transformed her tremendously, especially in the beginning of having to leave her home and reevaluate her finances and living situation. It was all very intriguing to me and our situations did seem to parallel each other. Dana turned out to be such a nice lady and I could really use a new friend at that time, so I decided to join her for the next IANDS meeting the following Saturday at 2 P.M. There was no charge for attending and you could give a donation of their suggested $20 if you wished, but it was not necessary. I had no idea that Dana, by exposing me to psychics, mediums, NDEs and IANDS, would change my life and open up an entirely new way of making sense of the universe. It was as if she was an Angel sent by God to reach out to me during the early stages of my life change. You see, the garage sale was a fairly preliminary hurtle in the changes and experiences that I had yet to face.

My first IANDS event was amazing and personally life altering. In fact, I would call it a watershed moment in my life. I love describing an event as a watershed moment. It reminds me the Atlanta-based Grammy Award-winning folk rock duo Indigo Girls with Amy Ray and Emily Saliers. Their lyrics, melodies and harmonies are amazing, and the song "Watershed" seems appropriate for keeping positive through this garage sale: "Up on the watershed. Standing at the fork in the road. You can stand there and agonize 'til your agony's your heaviest load. You'll never fly as the crow flies. Get used to a country mile. When you're learning to face the path at your pace, every choice is worth your while." Well, I chose this path I'm on because I had to make a decision about the direction of my life. There will be bumps in the road, but I'm confident, especially with all these Spiritual signs at my garage sale, that goodness will prevail and peace, love and happiness will be mine. The event that day was a two-hour group reading presentation led by a famous East Coast psychic medium. Usually the IANDS meetings start with the microphone being passed to each person in each row where the attendees shared a quick bit on why they were there and if they had experienced an NDE. Often times folks would just nod and pass the microphone, but there were always the regulars who shared their same story over and over every month. This was usually followed by a guided group meditation with calming sitar or flute music playing in the background. This ritual was skipped this month because the organizers wanted to maximize the time of this well-known psychic medium. There were about one hundred attendees. Randomly, members from the audience were selected by the psychic medium to be recipients of a reading where their deceased loved ones gave them messages. The psychic medium had successfully read about six people who were shocked by his accuracy before somehow I was surprisingly selected. Well, now that I know what I know, there was probably nothing random about my being chosen. Once this psychic medium began providing not only the name but personal information about my Aunt Adeline, information that nobody but me knew and couldn't be Googled, I became immediately convinced of the integrity of what I was witnessing and experiencing.

I had already witnessed this psychic medium comfort shocked parents regarding their deceased son Treyvon by confirming that their son was in his twenties and had tragically died in a boating accident at the Morse Reservoir in Hamilton County where alcohol was a factor. The parents were told that they were to take care of his Dalmatian dog Buster (yes the psychic medium provided the exact cause and location of their son's death and his dog's breed and name). Their son was celebrating six months of sobriety so the parents questioned whether Treyvon had relapsed and gone off the wagon causing the accident, especially since the psychic medium mentioned that alcohol was involved. They were told that when Treyvon went out on his boat, he was unfortunately hit by another boater who was under the influence of alcohol and lost control, decapitating him as he was ejected, killing him instantly of course. His parents never said a word about the decapitation and couldn't believe the psychic medium knew about this gruesome detail that they couldn't get out of their "heads" (no pun intended). He told the parents that their son does not want them to remember how he died and what he looked like when they had to identify his body at the Hamilton County Morgue, but rather how he looked before the accident and what a wonderful life they had provided for him. Treyvon wanted his parents to know that he didn't relapse and that there was nothing they could have done differently and that he was happy now and at peace. Even though he had eventually mustered up the strength to beat his addiction to alcohol, he still had struggles in this life. As awful as it was to know this, the message was extremely healing for Treyvon's parents to hear. His parents now had a newfound sense of peace; even their posture and most definitely their ability to hold their heads up (again, no pun intended) and make eye contact were visibly improved than when they first walked into the IANDS meeting.

The miraculously accurate and spot-on readings continued. The specific details this psychic medium was able to relay to the loved ones of those who had transitioned were just mind-blowing, and they kept on coming. I witnessed another reading for a young lady. She was told that her fiancé was standing right behind her and that he knew she had his hat in her purse (she did!). He had died of a gunshot wound that went right through his left eye (he did!). She was also told that there was an ongoing investigation regarding his murder (there was!). She was also asked if October 5th meant anything to her. That was his birthday. Unbelievable! This was the real deal. If I had any doubts about the accuracy of the details before, I surely didn't now. The psychic medium went on to say that her fiancé was saying that he proposed to her at an Indian's baseball game (Oh my God, he did!) and he said that right after she said "yes" they were caught on the "Kiss Cam," which was the happiest day in his life. This specific evidence was not anything that could be looked up. This provided much desired proof that her late fiancé was with her now and loved her very much. Just as the focus was moving toward another Spirit, this young lady was told that her fiancé wants her to find love again and that it was okay to to use the large deposit on their reception at Mustard Seed Gardens to still have the big gathering with all their family and friends.

The psychic medium then went to this elderly man who was also in the same section of the audience, but a few rows in front of the young lady whose fiancé was murdered. The psychic medium said that this elderly man's wife was clambering her way in front of other spirits because she was "pushy" and needed to get a message to her husband. He explained that Spirits sometimes do this when they get an opportunity to communicate with someone who really needs it. The psychic medium asked the elderly man if a rose or roses meant anything to him. He replied that he couldn't think of any connection. The psychic medium insisted that what he was hearing from Spirit was accurate and it was clearly rose or roses. Nope. Nothing. Then he said that he could smell a perfume, which he was able to recognize as Avon's Sweet Honesty. The elderly man confirmed that his late wife, in fact, did wear Avon's Sweet Honesty, but he still couldn't account for the rose connection. He was able to confirm the other identifying clues which included canning pickles and crabapple jelly, wearing aprons, line-dancing, Thanksgivings at a Minnesota cabin and her volunteer work as a midwife assistant. The psychic medium asked her name and he replied "Anne," however then the elderly man's face lit up as he stated that her middle name was Rose; the mystery Rose connection was solved. Witnessing the messages relayed by this psychic medium was absolutely amazing. How could this complete stranger know all these intimate details from these audience members' loved ones? Then without any warning, it was my turn. Out of the large number of people at the meeting, I surely wasn't expecting to have a reading or to have my belief system permanently changed.

The psychic medium walked across the room to the back section where I was sitting. He said that there was an older, motherly figure named Adeline who was coming through. He asked if that made sense to anyone in the general vicinity. As I began to raise my hand and stand up, I noticed that there was a man a few rows over who was also standing up. My beloved paternal Aunt Adeline had passed away a month prior. I became close to her the past five years or so. I really felt a desire to connect with her growing up, but we never really talked much. Whenever there were family get-togethers, the adults would all sit in the front parlor talking and smoking while the kids were all sent outside to the "back forty" to play kickball or paint with water on those amazing coloring books that when you add water to certain sections, the grey newsprint would change to one of the primary colors. My Aunt Adeline was a pretty quiet and reserved relative in general. She was the only girl in a family with five other boys, plus she was much older than her brothers. She would always refer to her brothers as "The Boys." All of her brothers were professionally accomplished and Ivy-League scholars. My dad was an Emeritus history college professor and my four uncles' held the elite professional positions of federal judge, bank president, neurosurgeon and senator. My Aunt Adeline was expected to stay home after high school and help raise her five brothers. If my aunt would have gone to college it may have positively altered her life; her self-esteem would have most likely improved because she would have received a taste of some of the attention and accolades that her brothers had earned and enjoyed their entire lives. First of all, it was a very rare phenomenon back then for a woman to even go to college, let along pursue a Masters or Doctorate degree. Women in her generation did not have the opportunities or choices that women have in today's world. It was a common practice in her era for women to get married and raise a family. Period. That was their expected sole purpose in life and that is what Aunt Adeline did. She had two children: a boy and a girl, the scenario that parallels the currently held belief of the American Dream with the expected 2.5 children and the white picket fence, except for the added, "bring home the bacon, fry it up in a pan, and let your man know he's a man," so a few more responsibilities were added over the years for women to supposedly "have it all."

Aunt Adeline's daughter, my cousin Victoria, and I were not very close. There was an age difference, as she was nine years older than me, but it was the resentment I sensed that she seemed to have whenever our family was around her family that caused the lack of comradery. I later found out she was ordered by her parents to keep track of and babysit my two brothers and me. We were considered "wild children," not brought up with the specific manners and the proper etiquette that was expected of children when they were in the company of others. I'm sure we were a handful to chase around and try to control. Our parents were liberal and believed children should be independent and have freedom. They did not supervise us much or were strict by any means. Assigning mandatory babysitting duties to an older cousin by her mother would not lend itself to positive interactions and future feelings of connectedness. Victoria's younger brother Thomas had tragically passed away at the very young age of 15. He was in some accident where he was caught in the next-door neighbor's silo on the farm when he was helping them out and the silo was being filled with grain. He was alone when he was trapped in the silo as it was being mechanically filled and there was no chance of his survival. Even in the remote possibility that someone actually witnessed the accident and was close by, it would have been unlikely that they would have been able to dig him out in time. It was several days before his family and the authorities even entertained the idea that Thomas could have got trapped in and died in the silo. This was a very sad and awful situation, not just because his life on earth was cut short and the earthly world tragically lost a fine young man, but that the family had to deal with his death in silence. You see, back then, at least in their family, one was not to speak of or even think about death or tragedies such as this. Our grandmother's response was to say that there was nothing anyone can do about it now, so just forget that this happened and move on with your life. Nowadays there are supports in place to help people deal with losses such as this. There are researched and identified stages of grief to help people understand their emotions and cope. There are grief counselors and there are grief support groups, community outreach forums, books, classes and video blogs. Back then, grieving people suffered in silence. In fact, even the next door neighbors who owned the silo and who were previously very close with my Aunt and her family stopped talking to her after the accident. You would think they would be there to comfort and support each other, but that was not the case. So not only did my Aunt Adeline lose her son, in a sense, she also lost her best neighbor friend, and life as she knew it would never be the same.

I remember the exact time when my relationship with Aunt Adeline deepened. I was home from college and we were in the parked car in my parent's driveway and we just talked. I had never really had a conversation with my aunt. What was very significant was that we talked about the death of her son, my cousin, which had happened many years before. I told her that I didn't really remember Cousin Thomas that well, as we never played together when our families would gather for the annual holiday feast. It was as if a dam broke and opened up and my aunt was given permission to express emotions that she had kept buried deep within her heart and soul for so many years. My aunt really talked in detail about Thomas, not just about his death, but mostly about his life while he was here on this earthly plane those short 15 years. She told me her religious beliefs; a topic that was never part of any family discussions in my childhood. She was a devoted member of the Unity Church. She said she was a strong believer in reincarnation and life after death. She believed that someday she would be reunited with her son Thomas in the Afterlife. I paid close attention to her words, even though it seemed she was speaking a foreign language. I didn't really understand her beliefs because they were so vehemently different than those of my parents, but I was open-minded and really wanted know her perspective. Ever since that conversation in the parked car, my relationship with my Aunt Adeline was deepened.

Our relationship continued to grow over the years. I felt close to my Aunt Adeline and I knew that she felt close to me. In her later years I would make extra efforts just to see her and spend time with her. Her husband had passed away and because of medical issues, she moved in with her daughter, my cousin Victoria. Victoria followed the family's expectations and took on the role of taking care of her mom. When I would visit my aunt, I really looked at it as visiting my aunt alone, so I never really spent much time or talked much with my cousin Victoria. I flew out a couple of times a year to spend time with my Aunt Adeline. She and her daughter lived in the town of Nixa, Missouri. It was close to Branson, while naturally beautiful in landscape and scenery, the area was very isolated and was actually a tacky entertainment town for the old, non-A-listers to continue their life of performing. Branson was about a 25 minute drive from Nixa if there was no traffic or an ice storm, and it had just opened up an airport of its own, however not many flights were set up; that would have been way too convenient. Instead, I was able to fly from Indianapolis, Indiana to Springfield, Missouri and then rent a car and make my way to my aunt's within an hour-long drive. Our visits were great and our relationship went from feeling like a family obligation to sincerely loving and friendly. One very special visit was when I flew out to see her and stay with her at her friend's Bed and Breakfast named "The Seasons." It was like a girls' weekend. I had my suitcase filled with surprises and activities for us to do together during our visit. I brought a large puzzle for us to work on, all of the craft supplies to make flower pens and fleece material in red and purple to make a beautiful "Red Hat Club" tie blanket. I thought these activities would be conducive for being able to talk with one another while we were using our creative handiwork skills to complete some fun projects. I even bought us matching nightgowns, socks, slippers, coffee mugs and pillow cases. I planned a spa afternoon with do-it-ourselves mani-pedis and facials. This weekend provided a bit of a break for my cousin Victoria, who mainly served as my Aunt Adeline's caretaker. At one point, though, I had to call Victoria for assistance when my aunt's feet began to turn purple from my massaging them. I really didn't know what to do and panicked. It turned out that she was O.K. She just needed her feet and legs elevated for an hour or so. Other than that, this particular visit was one of the best times I had ever spent with my Aunt Adeline, and now she was coming through in my reading by this very spot-on psychic medium.

So there I was, along with this other audience member, an elderly man, standing in anticipation of hearing from one of our departed Adelines. Whose Adeline would it be? Mine or his? Then the psychic medium said that Adeline's Spirit was with a man. We both still stood standing. He went on to describe this other Spirit as a man who was very stocky with a roughness about him, and that he was smoking a cigar. The elderly gentleman sat down because clearly this description didn't resonate with his Adeline. My aunt's husband was stocky and smoked cigars. The psychic medium continued to provide a great deal of proof so that this evidence would be the confirmation that I needed to know that it was really her. This experience was surreal. Could my departed aunt really be communicating from across another dimension? Time sort of stood still as more and more evidence was brought forth. Oh my gosh! I was one of the few lucky recipients of an actual psychic medium reading! Of course, a part of me still questioned this entire experience, but I was open and honestly there were too many accurate comments that nobody else would have known for me to question the validity of this reading. This information could not be looked up on a computer. Only I would know this information. The psychic medium asked me if I was working on a family tree project. I couldn't really think of one. He said that my Aunt Adeline is referencing something to do with genealogy. I thought about my aunt and couldn't really make a connection with her and genealogy. I had once helped her organize and publish the collection of her original poems, but I had not worked on genealogy with her. The psychic medium wouldn't give up trying to help me see the connection. Then he said that my Aunt Adeline wants me to complete the family tree project for my aunt from the other side of the family. Now this actually made sense! Just a week prior I went to Holly Springs, North Carolina to visit my 90 year old Aunt Ethel. She was one my mother's sisters and spent all of her free time researching various family names, history and connections. After a couple of days with her and a visit to the Green Lawn Memorial Gardens Cemetery to see the family plots of our deceased loved ones, my Aunt Ethel showed me numerous binders jam-packed with copies of documents supporting the research she had done on our maternal family lineage. It was a compilation of a lifetime of devotion and obsession by my Aunt Ethel. When I was in North Carolina visiting Aunt Ethel I was fascinated, not just by all of her hard work on genealogy, but by her patience and perseverance, along with her meticulous recording of details and dates. I wanted to help her become a published author with her work, just like I helped my paternal Aunt Adeline become a published author with her book of poetry. Of course, this family tree project I offered to help my Aunt Ethel with would have to be simplified, a scaled-down version; a short book that she could give her grandchildren to eventually give to their children and grandchildren. Aunt Ethel was thrilled of my interest and accepted my offer to compile and complete this project, especially since she didn't have anyone else in the family who was as enthusiastic about genealogy. Her son was more of a new-age digital guy, so any genealogical work he did utilized computer databases and Ancestry.com. Both of my aunts and myself are "hard copy" girls and we like the feel and function of an actual, tangible book. Together my Aunt Ethel and I picked out the title, photos and binding color. So let me get this straight: the psychic medium was telling me that my paternal Aunt Adeline was telling me to complete the family tree project for my maternal Aunt Ethel. Crazy!

Together in planning out her genealogy book, my Aunt Ethel and I took a photograph of some amazing tree roots from the one and only tree planted in her side yard. I was instructed to use this photograph on the cover along with the title "Our Family Roots." My aunt made a list of everyone who she wanted me to send the book to, including the local church and library and the genealogical organizations she was a member of. She was also a proud member of the DAR-Daughters of the American Revolution and called herself a "Colonial Dame," saying that our lineage goes back to the Mayflower. She whispered to me, as if she was sharing a devastating secret, that in our family we had a "negro" connection and that a distant uncle's slave gave birth to their illegitimate child. I was actually thrilled to hear this because of my liberal beliefs and open nature, but held in my enthusiasm as I know she was prejudice against anyone who didn't have white skin. Our visit turned out to have much more of a purpose to it now that she was relieved that her legacy and research would live on after her time on this earth ended. The psychic medium asked if I understood what my paternal Aunt Adeline was saying about finishing the family tree project for the other side of the family. Well, at this point I surely did see the connection and understood the message. I know now, and it has been further confirmed ten times over with other readings and Spiritual experiences, that life does continue after our physical death. How completely accurate! In fact, all of the readings I heard seemed to be completely accurate and resonate with those who were fortunate enough to have Spirit come through with messages. So, not only was I provided with evidence and proof that this after-death communication was the real deal, my life as I knew it would never be the same. I followed up with a mediumship workshop that weekend where I learned a lot about the process of trusting your intuition. At the end of the workshop I got yet another reading from a different psychic medium.

I enjoyed the mediumship/intuition exercises, but didn't really get the impression that I would have what it takes to successfully employ the skills required to speak to or hear from departed loved ones, let alone evoke the power needed to transcend into the Spiritual realm. Well, as it turned out, I was spot on in the workshop with all of my responses when the psychic medium asked us to use our different "Clares" to make connections. When I was asked to use clairvoyance to visualize one of his good friends and all I was given was the name, I immediately saw a white motor scooter, which was the only accurate response from the entire group. I was also told that I was completely accurate in another exercise when we were asked about a girl he was thinking of. We were supposed to use clairaudience to describe what we heard. I tried hard to focus on my hearing, but I told him that I only had a vision that this girl just broke her arm and that I had a feeling that her sister had just passed away. I shocked myself and other participants because I got both of these details correct. In yet another exercise, I apologized that I just couldn't focus on the emotions of the next scenario as we were asked to use clairsentience and that again I saw a vision. I told him that I visualized two scenes that felt to me like I was seeing a frame from a movie. I was encouraged to share what I saw. I saw a teenager with red curly hair and I saw that he had a wetsuit on and was about to embark on a diving expedition. I saw that he had an encounter with an octopus. The psychic medium confirmed that my visions were the specific details he was seeking. What was happening here? I had no idea how I was able to provide this correct information. This was weird. The other workshop participants were looking at me as if I had a magical power. Now for my reading. The psychic medium instructed me to stand. He asked if I had a brother who had transitioned. I confirmed that one of my two brothers had passed away. I was just about to volunteer validating information, but he stopped me and told me not to say anything confirming because it was not necessary as he was still hearing from Spirit. He was actively listening and even said, "O.K." aloud as if he was responding to the deceased loved one's Spirit communication. He asked if my brother's name was Harold. I nodded in affirmation. My jaw literally dropped as I couldn't believe he got my brother's name. He went on to say that Harold was mentioning Jane. (That was his wife.) He said that there was a mother figure with a name that begins with "E" looking over him. (Our late mother's name was Elaine.) He laughed and said that our mother was with him and doting on him. He told me Harold was very thankful and appreciative that I reached out to him to show my acceptance of his sexual orientation, and not just be tolerant or judgemental. Wow. This was again getting personal. This reading was shockingly precise. I had made a special effort years back to visit my brother Harold and hang out with him at the gay bars in his city; this was a real stretch for me as we never got along as kids and in my youth I had relentlessly teased him for his feminine qualities. I became somewhat embarrassed after high school when he "came out" announcing that he was homosexual. I thought of how, especially after his death, I was ashamed at myself for not accepting my brother for who he was. I pride myself (no pun intended) in now being overly accepting of individuals when it comes to race, religion, political views, education levels and gender preferences. Anyway, on this visit with Harold I tried to be open-minded about his chosen lifestyle, if in fact it was a choice. Most likely he was born this way.

As time went on, my brother and I didn't really stay in touch much. The animosity cement experienced in childhood seemed to have hardened, creating a permanent disconnect between us. Harold ended up marrying Jane, a very close girlfriend of his, even though he had previously celebrated a "Holy Union" with another man. I digress. Back to the reading. The psychic medium placed his hands around his neck and said that something Spirit will show is how the person died. In fact he often can feel physical pain in a part of his own body when Spirit is trying to give this information for evidence. For example, if he feels pain in the chest, that could indicate that the person died from a heart attack. If he mentions the feel of a smooth scalp and loss of hair, that might mean that the person passed away from cancer and lost their hair as a result of chemotherapy. With my brother Harold, the psychic medium asked if he took his own life by hanging. Harold had hung himself in the garage of the home he shared with his wife Jane. I replied, "He did." Again, I was floored by the validity of this information. He went on to say that even though his death was declared a suicide, he was actually hanging himself just to seek attention and did not intend to follow through with the act, but he slipped, broke his neck and died. By this time I was unable to hold in my emotions. I cried and shook as I tried to catch my breath. I was finally grieving the loss of my brother, especially knowing now that he really didn't want to end his life and that it was an accident. I was told that my brother Harold was at peace and watches over me.

I would never have learned about psychics, mediums, NDEs or IANDS if it had not been for that lady Dana, who coincidentally (or not) came to my garage sale and took the time to talk with me about all of this. She either was a messenger or an Angel. She had a huge impact on sparking my interest in Spirit and encouraging me to fan the flame of acknowledging the serendipitous experiences leading to my Awakening. Life and death as I knew it to be was not what I thought. I had so much confirmation of this. Dr. Weiss, in his book Many Masters Many Lives, believed that people go beyond their (what we call normal) limits of space and time. Maybe that is what has happened to me. I am forever grateful to Dana who approached me and started talking with me at my garage sale. It now feels that this meeting was synchronous and it just wasn't a coincidence that she was there because our conversation led to the amazing and life-altering topic of mystical experiences and IANDS. Was Dana just another shopper looking through other people's things for a deal? Was she a messenger or was she an Angel? Was I guided to attend the IANDS meetings? Was it chance that I got two very personal and accurate readings by famous psychic mediums? Did my Aunt Adeline and Aunt Ethel guide me during this time? Did my brother Harold orchestrate this? Did God come to my garage sale?

CHAPTER 6

The Aunts and The Angels

"Rocks and waters, etc. are words of God, and so are men. We all flow from one fountain soul, all are expressions of one Love."

John Muir

Scattered among the book section of my garage sale were six blank family tree books. They were the hardcover kind with lines and pages that were empty where you fill in the names of your relatives, dates and other important details such as your family members' interests and occupations. Why was I selling six of them? A better question was why did

I even own six of them? I guess I was collecting them in the hopes that I would be able to complete books for others. When I decided to straighten up the books, I thought about my aunts on both my mom and dad's sides. Almost immediately at my garage sale, on this hot summer day in July, a very unique cool breeze swept by my face. I remember it because the breeze seemed to come out of nowhere and was strong enough to blow my hair, yet the breeze only affected me and not anything or anyone else around me. No leaves or trees rustled. Only I felt it. I had heard stories of Guardian Angels making themselves known by cool breezes, but I didn't make that connection just then. I went about tidying up the book section hoping that I could sell at least half of the many books I had collected over the years. I had always been interested in genealogy, just like my Aunt Ethel. Ever since I was in high school I kept one of the books out and used it as a working copy to update whenever there was a birth, death or marriage in the family. I had a surge of increased interest in genealogy when I was in college and my maternal grandmother Janet (who I was named after (she was referred to as Big Janet and I was Little Janet) passed away. I flew from Indiana where I was in school to Florida to join my two brothers and mom at her funeral. It was there that my mom's sister, my Aunt Ethel, filled me in on the specifics of our family lineage. As I mentioned before, Aunt Ethel was a proud long-standing member of the DAR-Daughters of the American Revolution and puffed up with pride when she announced to me that both of us were considered to belong to the elite status of Colonial Dames. She had devoted her life to genealogy research and this was many, many years before there were computer searches and organizations that had family search databases whose efficient research tools make the gathering of family tree information much easier. I'll never forget when she specifically told me of her shame that we had "Negro blood" in our family line. Also, as I previously referenced, I consider myself to be open-minded and liberal regarding people's cultural backgrounds, especially when it comes to people's ethnicity or skin color. To Aunt Ethel's dismay, I was glad to hear of the more colorful and less "pure" tapestry of my lineage. I was still careful not to discuss my liberal thoughts too openly as I didn't want Aunt Ethel to stifle me or for her to stop telling me the sordid details of the mixed union or the illegitimate "Negro" child which I wanted to hear more about. It was hard, but I had to bite my tongue as she gave the information with her usual slant of prejudice. Aunt Ethel has since passed away and she would turn over in her grave if she knew that resulting from my own recent genealogical searches, I uncovered that our 44th United States President Barack Hussein Obama II is actually my 10th cousin, not even removed.

The next big surge of interest in my lineage which prompted me to conduct further research on my own was several months before my dad's 70th birthday. I was putting together a scrapbook of memories for him from his momentos, photos and newspaper clippings which he had saved over the years. In my lifetime I have assembled some amazing memory books for relatives, if I say so myself. One scrapbook that I was especially proud of was for my lovely maternal spinster Aunt Josephine, who we would call Aunt Jo. She was beautiful and very graceful. We would call her a "girly-girl." I was drawn to do something very special for her because she had never experienced a wedding or baby shower, even though over the years she had many suitors vying for her affections. She had always generously given gifts and cards to countless others for their momentous occasions. I decided to throw her a surprise 75th birthday party. I wrote to every family member and friend of hers. I asked them to please send me their photo and a special birthday letter. With love and care I collected them all and arranged them in a special padded photo album that I made and personalized especially for her, down to the floral and lace fabric that represented her interest and taste in frilly, feminine-style clothes. This surprise party and memory book gift for my Aunt Jo made her so very happy that she cried a river of tears. Aunt Jo did appreciate all of my efforts and told me that this surprise meant the world to her and that I was her "Earthly Angel." Me an Angel? Well, I did feel that I lived my life empathetically and took great joy in helping and caring for others. I was always an honest, upstanding and loving person with integrity. I was the only family member to ever to turn the spotlight on Aunt Jo. Finally. It seemed that nobody else in our family ever thought of doing such a thing. She never got much attention and it was always expected that she would be there with her gifts and cards at all the family's "doings." I really loved her. I spent a lot of time with Aunt Jo. I was the only one with whom she would feel comfortable when it came to some very personal bodily matters. Nobody likes to talk about it or certainly deal first hand with it, but Aunt Jo had lost the ability to control her bowels and would soil herself whenever

I took her out to a restaurant or department store. Aunt Jo was a very proud woman and not interested in wearing adult diapers. She felt more comfortable in her big, high-waisted, white, cotton "granny" underwear. I helped change her all the time. I bought packages and packages of 12-pack Hanes underwear, size enormous, at the local Walmart. She would use these cotton briefs as if they were her disposable diapers. It became very obvious when she was ready for a change; just like a baby when there was poop in the diaper, the smell was awful. And her walking around after she relieved herself made the mess even worse. I would change her and clean her up whenever she needed it. At first she was embarrassed and apologetic, but then she realized I was happy to help. She trusted me and only me to take care of her. She was very appreciative of her "Angel" and we formed a special bond from those intimate moments. Aunt Jo was most definitely with me in Spirit at my garage sale.

I believed that my dad would like to hear from people in his life while he was living and to be able to know their fond memories of him, especially because he was an Atheist and he didn't believe in any chance that there would be any type of connection after his death. In order to do this book of memories for my dad, I needed to contact anyone close to or related to him. One of my dad's brothers had already done a great deal of genealogy on his side of the family and had most everyone's name, location and contact information. I didn't have addresses, phone numbers or emails, but I knew that I had it in me to research and get my dad's family's contact information; my premium subscription to an online search database came in handy. I was able to talk with distant cousins that had not communicated with my dad since his childhood days. I believe that God had an even stronger purpose for me doing this project because I was again told I was an "Earthly Angel" and was extremely instrumental and timely in reuniting some relatives in the middle of a tragic life-and-death situation. My perseverance and patience in making call after call after call contributed to reuniting some of my dad's estranged family members during a critical emergency situation. You see, one of my dad's second cousins could not be reached because he was in the hospital literally clinging to his life. When I called his phone, a neighbor happened to be at his house checking on his dog who had been left alone for four days. Four days prior, my dad's second cousin had driven off the road down into a very steep ditch. He was trapped in the car for four very long days without any help whatsoever. It wasn't until a motorist needing to stop and change his car's tire noticed a car upside down in the ditch leading him to call the authorities for help. It was later discovered that the man in the overturned car was almost dead; that man was my dad's second cousin. After talking with this neighbor, who by chance was in this second cousin's house and answered my phone call providing me with details, that an amazing chain reaction of communication ensued. I was able to share this information with another second cousin's family, who had been estranged from him for years. They thanked me for the information, said that they would reconnect with him immediately, told me that I must have been an Angel sent by God to be at the right place at the right time and headed directly to the hospital. I felt that God guided me somehow to help aid in this man's life and reunification with his distant family members. If I had not chosen to put this memory book together for my dad when I did and kept steady and persistent with my efforts to connect with anyone I could, I wouldn't have been placed in the middle of learning about this accident and reuniting long lost loved ones with each other. There seemed to me to be a much higher purpose going on here. I felt God's intervention and guidance.

I was able to present the memory book with all of my dad's family tree information, photos and letters to him for his 70th birthday. My dad thanked me for the book. I had put so much time and love into it that I was taken aback when he really didn't seem to care about it much as he just flipped through the pages without even reading the letters before storing the scrapbook in his office closet. I didn't let him see that I was hurt. I didn't make a big deal about it and just told myself that it was not about the other person's reaction to my efforts, but the love I felt in creating and completing this momento. It wasn't until years later, when my dad was 84 years old and he was cleaning out his office and came across the memory book that he really took the time to peruse each page and read each letter that was written to him. Fourteen years after receiving the book it finally had significant meaning to him. My dad did eventually seem appreciative and made an effort to sincerely thank me then.

I was thinking about Aunt Ethel and Aunt Adeline, as well as Aunt Adeline's late son, my cousin Thomas, who had tragically died in that grain silo farm accident. I didn't even look up to see the person who was coming to check out and pay for the garage sale items they wanted to buy. Then I saw that the purchase included two of the family tree books. I raised my head and realized that it was a young boy buying the books. He seemed about the same age as my late cousin. "What a coincidence," I thought to myself. He also appeared to be from a farm, as he was wearing Oshkosh bib overalls and had a red bandana around his neck. I thought it was strange, not only for this boy to be dressed like he was from a country farm (of which there was none around here), but to be buying these books instead of items such as Legos, Indianapolis Colts memorabilia, skateboards and such, which would seem more suitable items for his age. I asked him why he was buying these family tree books. He told me that he had two aunts who were encouraging him to research his lineage, plus he had to do a major genealogy project and he could use the blank forms in the book for his report. After our transaction and as he was walking away I asked him his name. My jaw dropped as he replied, "Thomas." Was this Thomas kid reincarnated or sent supernaturally to my garage sale to buy my family tree books? Did I really feel the cool breeze of my Guardian Angel as I was thinking of my Aunt Ethel, Aunt Adeline and Aunt Jo? Were there some heavenly, mystical experiences at play here prompting me to think about my aunts? Did Spirit intervene with my dad's memory book or my acting on his second cousin's car accident reuniting estranged family members? Was there more going on here? Did God come to my garage sale?

CHAPTER 7

The Old Man in The White Suit

"Let us aspire towards this living confidence, that it is the will of God to unfold and exalt without end the spirit that entrusts itself to Him in well-doing as to a faithful Creator."

William Ellery Channing

My 8th grade English teacher at Brownsburg West Middle School was a very old, very tall, very smart and very patient man named Mr. Argent. Between classes or before and after school Mr. Argent would stand outside of his classroom door. He appeared to almost touch the ceiling. He always had a very gentle demeanor. Even though he seemed ancient, his personality was very welcoming and approachable to junior high-aged kids who had inner pre-teen angst and turmoil despite their calm, cool and collected outward personas. We preteens craved peer acceptance as we navigated the daily school routines and unwillingly accepted the structure of this new experience of moving rooms and changing teachers for each class. Mr. Argent was a bright spot in my day. I remember him as if my middle school experience was yesterday. One of my best friends Lina and I would approach Mr. Argent on a daily basis by asking him in unison, "Mr. Argent, how is your day going?" He would always smile and reply with a gentle nod and a one-word answer, "Fine." Then we would always come back with our usual second statement, "You have a nice bow tie on today." Mr. Argent always wore bow ties. A memorable customer at my garage sale was a very tall, old man in a white suit. I did a double-take because he reminded me so much of my middle school teacher Mr. Argent. I saw the old man in the white suit drive up to my cul-de-sac and park his vintage, white Cadillac at the end of my driveway. As he got out of his car I noticed that his movements were very slow and calculated, yet strong and definitive. He was most likely in his nineties. He was formally dressed in white from head to toe and wore a white bow tie. He was healthy-looking, yet I could tell his skin was thin and crepe-like. His blue eyes, however, appeared very youthful and had a unique sparkle and twinkle in them. He gestured and tipped his white top hat in lieu of a verbal greeting of "Good morning." I don't think that I had ever seen anyone wear a top hat. I continued setting out items without approaching him, as I assumed he wanted to take a look at what I had for sale. The old man in the white suit walked around very slowly. I was trying not to think about the house and life I was leaving behind. Most of the items I was discarding were once either functional and needed or played a role in the house decor I was compelled to surround myself with, periodically changing and updating as my style, tastes and trends changed. Of course, I know now that money and things can't buy you love. Just then I looked up and noticed that the old man in the white suit had pulled up a chair and sat down right next to me.

In his hands were three picture frames. I stopped what I was doing to ask if he had any questions about the frames. My interactions with him seemed to be in slow motion and suspended in time. I know I was talking with him, but it felt like it took me an hour to finish one sentence. This was weird. I wasn't sure about what was going on and I really didn't expend the energy or take the time to question it. At the same time, I was aware that something out of the ordinary was happening. It reminded me of those old Batman reruns where the Penguin or Joker would enter a room and the unknowing crowd of innocent bystanders would be paralyzed and frozen in time while the conniving criminals would walk around unaffected by the trance. It was like I was in a time warp. I asked the old man in the white suit if he had questions about the frames in his hands. He said "No." So maybe he just needed to rest; he was very old and most people I see that old need to stop and take things slower. Usually Midwesterners start off conversations talking about the weather, especially when you are talking with people you don't know, however, the old man in the white suit and I began talking about animals. Over the years my children and I had acquired two pugs, two guinea pigs, one Betta fish and many other creatures in our "zoo." I have always loved animals and had a strong interest and connection with animals. I was constantly rescuing various animals that would find themselves on our property, including birds, snakes, deer, groundhogs, turtles and stray cats. Every animal and rescue mission brought a sense of connection to the global community of all things living. I found satisfaction and purpose when tending to or helping animals. The old man in the white suit and I seemed to talk for hours, just sitting there alone in my driveway. We talked about my pugs and my brother Wade's beloved Australian Shepherd dog Fiona. I didn't share with him that Fiona was three-legged as a result of having her leg amputated after she was savagely mauled by another dog. What happened next was like a scene out of "The Twilight Zone."

The old man in the white suit began to talk about three-legged animals and how very special they were; this was without any knowledge about my brother Wade's dog Fiona and the fact that she had only three legs. He talked about how these three-legged animals are very special to God and that they are very strong, not just being able to stand without the support of a fourth leg, but just in their ability to adapt to life considering their doggy disability. He talked about how much love their human owners have for their pets, often electing to have costly surgery as opposed to thinking that losing a leg would be justification for putting them down and supposedly out of their misery. He shared with me that he has never owned a dog and favors cats as pets. I told him that I really didn't know that much about cats and favor dogs. His current cat was an outdoor cat who lost her hind leg from a run-in with some other animal when she was out in the "back forty" of his property. He said he was very partial to his three-legged cat and that in return, his cat seems to show a great deal of fondness for him, as if the cat's mobility challenges contributed to a certain deep love for the fact his owner takes such good care of him. The old man in the white suit looked me straight in the eyes and said, "You know, all pets, including three-legged ones, always go to Heaven." Was he trying to quote that 1989 Disney movie "All Dogs Go To Heaven?" I again thought it was odd that the old man in the white suit was referencing three-legged animals, not knowing that I was Aunt Janet to my brother Wade's three-legged Aussie. I loved Fiona, the Australian Shepherd, as if she was my own pet. My brother would tell me that just the mention of my name would excite Fiona. I thought that she got riled up from being conditioned by my always bringing her a toy and a marrow bone with every visit. In December, Fiona would get even more toys and treats because we celebrated the holidays of Christmas, Hanukkah, Kwanzaa and New Year's plus her birthday. The next thing that happened was yet another affirmation of the mystery surrounding this garage sale visitor, the old man in the white suit.

My brother Wade drove up with his dog Fiona, opened the car door and instead of coming over to me like she always did, Fiona ferociously wagged her tail and excitedly hobbled over on her three legs directly to greet the old man in the white suit. This was so odd because Fiona is actually a very cautious dog and usually shys away from strangers. She acted like she had known this man for years and years. The old man in the white suit reached into his coat pocket and pulled out a dog toy and a large marrow bone and gave it to Fiona in the same way that I would have done. "This seems so odd," I thought. Why would this man, who just got through telling me he has a cat and has never had a dog, have a dog toy and marrow bone in his pocket? The old man in the white suit and his obvious three-legged friend, my brother's dog Fiona, had an instant connection, as if they had previously known each other extremely well. After another few minutes or so I realized that the old man had vanished without a trace and without any warning or parting pleasantries. I don't remember the man leaving at all. The last thing I remember was him giving Fiona the toy and bone. Did I just imagine the whole thing? No, I couldn't have. I looked down at Fiona and she was lying peacefully next to her new dog toy and was enjoying her marrow bone, so he had to have been there. After spending so much time at the garage sale with me, you would have thought the old man in the white suit would have at least said "Goodbye" or something, especially since we exchanged such a nice conversation and seemed to have that deep connection with the coincidental three-legged pet situation. I would have seen him drive away in his oversized white Cadillac because he was parked right at the end of the driveway, however his car was nowhere to be found. He was gone. I became confused. This was all a blur.

As I sat down, my shock regarding this encounter became even more unbelievable when I recounted that the man had a dog toy and marrow bone in his pocket and gave it to Fiona, my brother's three-legged dog, even though he doesn't even have a dog, only a cat, who happens to also be three-legged. Then I remembered Fiona's behavior and how she always comes to me, her Aunt Janet. Yet, this time, she bypassed me to greet this stranger. Was he a stranger? I asked my brother what he thought and he looked at me like I was crazy. My brother said that there was no old man in a white suit driving a white car that gave Fiona a toy and bone. He suggested that I was seeing things and that I must be under a great deal of stress. I know what and who I saw was real. Then, I thought about my 8th grade English teacher, Mr. Argent. I realized that the old man in the white suit who came to my garage sale may have been Mr. Argent's Spirit. They looked the same and acted the same. The garage sale customer even wore a bow tie just like Mr. Argent; I remembered that detail because these days it's rare to see someone in a bow tie. Some people still wear bow ties. One of the most talented folk musicians of our times, singer/songwriter Livingston Taylor, wears bow ties. As a full professor at the largest independent college for contemporary music in the world, Berklee College of Music in Boston, Massachusetts, Liv teaches a class with the same title as his best-selling book, Stage Performance. With his unique style and dry sense of humor, in addition to valuable lessons in music, he instructs students on the art of captivating an audience by carefully untying his bow tie. Was this bow-tied man Mr. Argent? No, it couldn't have been. Mr. Argent was the oldest person I knew and that was back thirty five years ago or so. He couldn't have still been alive. Plus, teachers usually remember their students, even if it had been years and years since they have seen them. He surely would have remembered me and said something. No, it couldn't have been him, but the similarities were uncanny. Plus, the way he just disappeared didn't seem like a Midwestern way to part company. Just then, even though the radio wasn't even on, the start of Josh Groban's song "To where are you are" came blaring out of the radio. I clearly heard the beginning words as if they were sung in slow motion: "Who can say for certain? Maybe you're still here. I feel you all around me. Your memory is so clear. Deep in the stillness. I can hear you speak. You're still an inspiration. Can it be?" These words had so much meaning and we're so very timely, as if to be giving me a message. But how could the radio just turn on by itself?

A slow, mystical and confusing feeling overwhelmed me. Wade and I sat down again on the lawn chairs in the driveway, with Fiona nestled on the blacktop below us. Wade allowed me to discuss and replay the events over and over, even though I am sure that he thought I was out of touch with reality. Maybe I was out of touch with reality, but I know what I saw and experienced. I wish I had had another witness, someone who saw and experienced the same thing that I did to confirm what just happened. Trying to explain this to someone who wasn't there and didn't see what I saw, along with all the personal and unique connections, would prove to be very difficult, not only to put into words but to have my experience accepted and understood. Was the old man in the white suit my 8th grade English teacher Mr. Argent? Was I hallucinating? Was he a Spirit? Was my brother Wade's three-legged Fiona involved in this mystery? Did God come to my garage sale?

CHAPTER 8

The Transgendered Tattoos and The Red Cardinals

"While I know myself as a creation of God, I am also obligated to realize and remember that everyone else and everything else are also God's creation."

Maya Angelou

Judging people by their appearance or by their sexual orientation is a terrible thing to do in my opinion. I have to admit it, though, that I have been guilty of previously passing judgement on others just as I know that I have been the recipient of someone else's negative judgement at one time or another. It has been said that people tend to make a snap perceptions about others within seconds of seeing them. I am and have always been accepting of people's sexual orientation, well, except for my brother Harold, but that was when I was younger. When it came to the issue of people having tattoos, it most likely was subconscious, but for most of my life I had a strong opinion and was very negative and judgemental. I was previously of the belief that the only people who had tattoos were either men that served in the military or motorcycle gang members who strut around in fringed, black leather sleeveless vests. Boy (no pun intended) things have evolved in our society and fortunately my earlier strong, misguided opinions have not only softened, they've done a 360. I like to think of myself as a very accepting and open individual. I was raised by very liberal parents during the 1960's. My parents bought me the book and record/LP Free To Be You And Me by Marlo Thomas and Friends that celebrated gender diversity among other progressive and less talked about social/emotional interpersonal issues. Being so closely connected to a college campus because of my dad being a college professor, I was exposed to people of all races, cultures, religions and sexual orientations, much more than my peers. My own brother Harold identified himself as gay in his youth and later bisexual. He even had a Holy Union ceremony that our 92 year old grandmother attended where in the service numerous gay relationships were referenced from the Bible. Unfortunately, at the young age of 41, Harold took his own life after years of emotional turmoil regarding his identity, along with succumbing to the devastating effects of the disease AIDS-Acquired Immune Deficiency Syndrome. I held tremendous guilt for the many times in our childhood that I bullied and teased my brother Harold about being gay. I still carry shame and regret my actions and behavior in my youth. As an adult, I distinctly remember that even though I was accepting of Harold, I wrongly invaded his privacy when I asked if he actually even had sexual relations with his (female) wife Jane of six years; that was very out of line for me.

Talking about sexual orientation is still taboo in the military. In fact, there are ongoing and changing legal policies that impact qualification of transgendered or other individuals with regard to military enrollment and service. Often the rights of more vulnerable people in our society are not held up in the legal system of our country, whether it's the injustice of the family court system, the deceitful and greedy lawyers or the mistreatment of minorities, including those that don't neatly and traditionally see themselves as either male or female. Places of employment have many challenges too, such as providing equal opportunities, pay, protocols and facilities. There are now multiple ways to identify yourself sexually; it's not just male, female, bisexual or gay. It's about the sense of being male or female or a combination, as well as who a person is drawn to physically, sexually and romantically. My own mother related more to women than men; I vaguely remember that she may have had a same-sex relationship at one point in her life, but of course, that wasn't acceptable to talk about openly at that era. Thankfully, both my mother's and my brother's Spirits came through loud and clear in a reading from an accomplished and well-known psychic medium. I am now more accepting of people's gender identities and tattoos, both of which I struggled with a bit when I was younger. I currently also sport two tattoos and have joined the masses who express themselves and have personal reasons for permanently inking the largest organ of their bodies. Young adults, and older ones like me, are becoming more empowered, open and honest these days with regards to sexual orientation and tattoos. And that's just part of it; there are legal and societal ramifications and rights that have needed to be addressed to ensure equality personally and professionally. Alfred Kinsey, in 1940, developed a scale (0-6) for measuring sexual orientation, however, it has taken many years to affect a change of attitude in our society. More recently, Cornell University psychology professor emeritus Ritch Savin-Williams researched the population he labeled as "straight with a bit of gayness." There are fairly new terms to address the categorizing of people and how they identify themselves with regards to their sexuality. Sexual identification and preferences are now being redefined and advocacy groups such as the GSA-Gay Straight Alliance and GLAAD-Gay & Lesbian Alliance Against Defamation are providing support and making their progressive marks on society. Celebrities in the arts, film and music industries have publically "come out" (of the closet) and now there are T.V. shows, movies, songs and advertisements showing more open and accepting depictions of options with regards to human sexuality. Before comedian, sitcom actress and talk show host Ellen DeGeneres "came out" there was an American sketch comedy T.V. show Saturday Night Live character named Pat, who was an androgynous fictional character created and performed by Julia Sweeney that later was the star of a feature film. Singer Katy Perry "Kissed A Girl and She Liked It" and Lady Gaga was "Born This Way." Cher and the late Sonny Bono's daughter is now their son. Bruce Jenner is now Kat. There are still discussions about whether sexual orientation and gender identities are a product of genetic predisposition or choice or a combination of both. Nature or nurture. And then there's the issue of matching anatomy, chromosomes and hormones, as well as societal expectations and individual expressions. There will always be those narrow-minded individuals that, sometimes in the name of God or religion, are against the pride (no pun intended) of diversity and who can be called homophobic. Social Media can often play a role in whether people find positive acceptance and learn that they are not alone in their feelings or they are negatively ridiculed and put down for their beliefs and behaviors. Cyber bullying is rampant and people are losing their lives to tragic circumstances such as murder and suicide as a result of discrimination. Rainbow ribbons are worn at Pride parades and rainbow flags (now in Philadelphia with two new stripes of black and brown to highlight members of the LGBT-QIA community-adding queer or questioning, intersex and asexual or allied) can be seen waving right next to the American flag. We still are a culture of labels. There are: PANs-pansexuals, aromantics, bi, asexual, genderqueer, non-binary trans, gender fluid and two-spirited. Not everyone is Cisgender, where their gender is in line with the sex they were assigned. Facebook even has over 50 options for a user's gender. There is, however, most definitely a generational gap on understanding and accepting these changes.

New York City has a law that now legally permits what is referred to as Generation X, where parents can modify and control the sex recorded at their baby's birth and have the right not to label their newborn as a boy or girl on their birth certificate, allowing the children to decide their own sex when they come of age. This, undoubtedly, will cause many changes to numerous other legal documents such as drivers' licenses, passports and social security cards. Bills and legislation are being introduced that add a third gender option of "non binary" on major documents such as birth certificates and driver's licenses. Many languages would have to be altered, namely the French "une" versus "un" for verb conjugation; boy, I mean girl, I mean "X," I wish that were the case back when I was taking French class in middle school because I always messed up on when to use the feminine "une" versus the masculine "un." Most languages use gender-specific pronouns, such as "he" and "she" and "his" and "hers," so human verbal and written language would be globally impacted. Airport security screening will have to be revamped; in India and other foreign countries you have only two choices of lines to go through: Gents and Ladies. Currently, there are lawsuits in the public schools regarding gender-related issues, often having to do with the closed policy regarding the use of and access to locker rooms or restrooms. The high school my children went to is even changing the tradition of nominating a King and Queen for homecoming and prom because that can now be viewed as discriminating. The internet and social media have been instrumental in spreading awareness. Sometimes labels can provide relief to those needing validation or acceptance, especially if they are in the mode of fluidity or changeability. Some individuals refer to themselves as "we" as opposed to "I" and "they" as opposed to "he" or "she." The LGBTQ community, loosely defined as people who identify as lesbian, gay, bisexual, transgender and queer or questioning has now been expanded with the times. Bob Dylan's 1964 song "The Times They Are a Changin'" is still applicable today. At the website www.lovehasnolabels.com it is stated that, "before anything else, we're all human. Rethink your bias." There are "ink" tattoo shows on T.V. Coworkers have after-work office group tattoo parties instead of the previously-practiced Happy Hours at the local pubs or pizza joints. Teenagers are asking their parents for tattoos as their main birthday gift. Mothers and daughters solidify their bonds by getting tattoos together and lovers continue to seal-the-deal with permanent proof of their commitment to one another, making tattoo removal a now lucrative business as relationships don't always take long term. Some individuals have an addiction related to getting tattoos and proceed to cover their entire body with these permanent embellishments. Still with the general acceptance of and widespread proof that tattoos have morphed into a mainstream, generational standard, it still wasn't anything I thought I would ever do to my skin or body, until my getting a tattoo would mean saving my nephew's life.

You see, my twenty-something nephew Preston was suffering from addictions. He had one enabling parent, my sister-in-law, with deep pockets who kept the perpetual cycle of dependence on substances going with financial handouts including paying his rent, phone, cable, insurance and living expenses along with those of his drug-using girlfriend, who had never experienced such a big and reliable meal ticket in her life. My nephew's mother never allowed him to flourish and develop the physical and emotional independence to be able to make it on his own independently, as most parents encourage and help their children work towards. Preston's friends may have dabbled in substances on a more social or experimental level, but never took it to the next serious step like he did. Preston moved out West to Ogden, Utah from the Midwest, originally to attend Weber State University. He wanted to go to college on a lacrosse scholarship, but those were only offered at colleges in the East. He was out of sight and out of mind for the enabling and controlling mom. My brother Wade, on the other hand, was the loving, empathetic, encouraging and present parent that believed in honest communication, healthy family relationships, fostering growth, positive self-esteem and you-can-make-it-on-your-own independence with hard-work and grit without enabling handouts. For almost three years, during the most challenging of times when my nephew Preston was in Utah, I was the relative he usually called on for emotional and loving support. Well, there was one extremely heartbreaking and critical moment when my nephew Preston called me and we spoke on the phone. I think he was afraid to call his parents. I knew something was terribly wrong this time. He was calling from some two-word town that started with the letter C. He was in another state further west than where he had been. He was no longer in Utah; now he was in some Portland, Oregon suburb. Our phone conversations usually lasted 20-30 minutes, but this time, this particular call was going on for over an hour. He wasn't making sense, although I didn't feel that he was in the middle of being high. This was more of a mental breakdown. His thought patterns seemed very disconnected from reality. Listening to him was actually very scary for me; I felt in my core soul that he was in serious danger and could do something to himself that would have devastating, lifelong negative consequences. I asked him if he called his parents, but he told me he couldn't talk with them or he would be in trouble. I was extremely thankful that we continued to share a loving, open relationship and he chose to call his Aunt Janet. Maybe on some level he knew that I wouldn't yell at him, tell him how negative his choices were and dictate the steps he would need to take to change to be a more appropriate and upstanding young man. He knew my love for him was "to infinity and beyond" and I would be able to help him somehow regain his footing in reality, maybe because he knew of my medical background as a nurse and that I've helped people in the hospital who were drugged up and out of it. Preston was hallucinating and delusional. He was describing the grass on the lawn and how the grass communicated with him. He also talked about the salmon from the local fish hatchery leaping out of the water in unison as a reaction to a John Mayer song that was playing in his head. I later learned that visions of jumping fish were part of what Harvard neurosurgeon Eben Alexander saw when he had his NDE. I know this sounds like someone who is high, but I also knew, as his aunt, that the problem was deeper than that. I knew I needed to make a trip out to Oregon and I had to do it immediately. In our hour-plus long conversation, Preston told me of being kicked out of three different tent communities. Who could get kicked out of homeless housing? Well, apparently he could. He also said that his car broke down and he had been living in an abandoned cabin, deep in the woods off the highway for the last three weeks. He is really bad this time. I told him I was going to come out to see him and take him to the hospital for a flu shot because I cared about his health. I actually just needed to get him to a hospital. Any real explanation for my visit may have been possibly met with opposition. He agreed that he would go with me for this immunization. Phew. Now I needed to get to him. Just then the phone disconnected and I was unable to reach him. Time to act.

I got special permission from the hospital I was working as a nurse at to leave immediately to get on the next plane to find my nephew. This was an emergency. I knew I was flying to Oregon, but I had no idea what town to go to, only that the two-word town began with the letter C and was a suburb of Portland. I tried to gather as much information as I could when I was on the phone with him; I knew he mentioned the town, but for some reason I couldn't remember it and now I had to just make an educated guess. I was filled with so much adrenaline and had no room for any friends or family to question my motives or persuade me to reconsider my plan, so I didn't tell anyone except my brother Wade what I was doing or where I was going, not even my dad, best friend, hospital coworkers or friends. Only the head physician and my brother Wade knew the details. The flight went so fast, probably because my mind was racing with concern and questions. I picked up my rental car and started driving to the first town that was nearby, a town called Cedar Mill. It didn't seem like a town where the homeless and down-and-out would hangout, but then again, just like tattoos and transgendered individuals, "you can't judge a book by its cover." Amongst this well-to-do metropolis was a shady underground of troubled folks. I parked the car and walked around for almost an hour. Unbelievable! I spotted my nephew Preston! He was not well. I have never seen his face the way it was. I don't even really have the words to describe what he looked like. His features seemed to be contorted. His eyes were like slits that rode up the sides of his face. Taking a closer look I saw that his pupils were extremely thin and long, and as a nurse I knew this was an indication of opiate use. I came armed with Narcan, which is short for Naloxone (an opioid antagonist used to reverse the effects of drug overdose) which all nurses are trained in to use. I had met the sister of a young addict who accidentally killed himself from his recreational drug use when this sister came to the hospital I work at and gave a presentation on the dangers of drug use and misuse. I later sought out her support to deal at a distance with how I can help and support Preston who had turned to this unhealthy, self-medicating coping behavior.

Preston was surprised to see me, even though during our conversation and before the phone was disconnected I told him that I was coming out to visit him and he agreed to let me take him for a flu shot. He was glad that his parents weren't there. My brother and I had actually already spoken with an intake specialist at the Providence Inpatient Psychiatric Care, right next door to the Providence Portland Medical Center and filled them in on the concerns I had regarding Preston, his substance abuse and current psychiatric delusions. I was able to quickly book a hotel, now that I confirmed the town he was in. He was thrilled to be able to take a hot shower with fresh, clean, white towels to dry off with. His clothes were disgustingly filthy, so I suggested I wash them and he just crawl under the covers for a good rest. This was much different than sleeping in an empty cabin for a month, which was hard to believe, but as I later found out turned out to be the truth. I thought he was sound asleep, so I left the hotel room, called Wade and filled him in on everything. I decided to run a few errands and put his super-soiled garments in the hotel washing machine as I went to Walmart to pick up a couple of changes of clothes for Preston. Big mistake. I learned that drug addicts can't be trusted at all. Turns out while I was gone Preston had ordered several room service meals, along with a six-pack of beer, which he managed to slam down. At least when I returned he was brutally honest with me and told me about it. Then he said that he needed to get a fix to get high. A fix? I never heard a young adult his age use those words, not even in the hospital. I pleaded with him not to, but he said he had to do it. It was hard for me to wrap my head around the idea of how he could have money for drugs, but not food and basic living necessities. Well, addicts find a way. Oh yeah, when they have an enabling parent who has no clue what is really going on and gives them cash and gift cards which can be exchanged for drugs and pay for their rent (even if they are living in a cabin which was free) and pay for gas and car insurance (even if their vehicle is inoperable and abandoned in the woods) and give them a Mastercard with no limit on it, I guess you have the money for drugs. I insisted that I go with him as he was "getting his fix" to see what he was doing. He didn't care. I saw it all, from the deal to the doing. It was hard to watch. Later that night I called my brother again to tell him the sordid details.

The next day Preston wanted to show me the fish hatchery that he had told me about on the phone and the outreach center that provided meals for him. Preston wanted me to drive to some highway where his car was hidden in the woods. Oh my God! When I saw the condition of his car I was just sick to my stomach; it was gross, with tires missing and doors taken off. There were hundreds and hundreds of cigarette butts sprawled out all over the interior. Neither my brother or I had any idea that he even smoked. Later on his mother criticized me and only seemed to care about the car and not her son's health and dire circumstances. Then Preston wanted me to drive my rental car a few miles down the road because he wanted me to meet someone. There was a roundabout on our drive and I slowed down because we really don't have many of those in Indiana and I wanted to make sure I could exit where I needed to. Preston's behavior as I entered this roundabout was alarming, to say the least. He started to shake and scream and ordered me to stop the car, which I did. He then proceeded to exit the rental car and run as fast as he could about 500 feet into the bushes. I put the hazard lights on and ran after him, afraid that he would get killed running into the highway traffic. I found him crouched down, shaking, rocking and crying. I gently walked him back to the car and we headed back down the road. I would later hypothesize that he must have had PSTD-Post Traumatic Stress Disorder because I had learned that he often sat in the middle of the road while cars sped by. He showed me the homeless tent community where he was no longer welcome. Preston felt the need to confront some guy that he had weeks before asked to watch his case of Gatorade. They started to get into a verbal altercation when the guy told Preston that he no longer had any of the drinks left. I mean really; who would save drinks for someone at a homeless tent community? As this was going on I chose to speak to a kind gentleman who I later found out was the volunteer social worker who oversaw the tent camp and seemed to have a positive working relationship with its transient residents. I told him of the main purpose of my visit and asked if he knew Preston. He sure did and said to me, "Ma'am, it is a major miracle that he is still alive." He thought I was his mom, but I told him I was his aunt and that his dad thought it would be best if I came out to rescue him because I was a nurse. My heart sank. The social worker told me about Preston's regular antics of going out onto the heavily trafficked expressway and sitting down between the lanes on the yellow solid do-not-cross line to get high; it sure was a miracle that he was still alive. Also another miracle was that he had not caused an accident or killed someone else with the many motorists who swerved to miss him as they were driving along and shocked to come across a crazy person with a death-wish risking everyone's safety. The social worker did say that Preston appeared to be a good person at one time, but he was definitely in crisis-mode now. On my way with him to go to the hospital to get his "flu shot" he asked me to pull over at this tattoo parlor to meet his friend, the owner who went by the name of Scrappy. My ingrained and long-held perceptions resurfaced and I made a negative judgement about the possibility that Preston's body was covered with tattoos. He said that he didn't have any tattoos. Wade had never mentioned he was into tattoos and the topic never came up during our family get-togethers. When we entered the storefront it was clear that Scrappy knew my nephew probably due to their drug connection. I didn't realize it then, but Scrappy played a large role in saving Preston's life that afternoon. Scrappy had a heart-to-heart talk with him and told him that in the many, many years of tattooing young adults who frequented his establishment, that he had never ever seen a relative as loving as me who would fly so far to save a kid, especially a kid that wasn't mine, and take them back home. Preston agreed and said, "Yep. My Aunt Janet loves me 'to infinity and beyond' and she came to get me and take me to the doctor." O.K. I will go with that. It surely wasn't my plan. I had planned to take him to the local hospital emergency room for an evaluation and detox, but here, without warning, was an opportunity to get him out of this state, back to Indiana and on the road to recovery. Oh my God! Thank you for answering my prayers. By Grace and Divine intervention, it appeared I was going to be able to somehow get Preston back home to his family in Indiana for help sooner than I had anticipated.

Scrappy said to my nephew that kids his age usually don't get a second chance at life; they either "end up incarcerated, trafficked, murdered or six feet under due to overdose." He could be one of the lucky ones. I don't know what possessed me, maybe it was the "location, location, location" and my extreme thanks for Scrappy's advice and convincing Preston to go home with me, but I blurted out, "Let's celebrate with a matching tattoo!" A big smile came over his face. Preston suggested that we both get Disney's Buzz Lightyear tattoos on our right shoulders because he said that he had fond memories of coming over to my house to watch Disney movies and that I would always tell him that I loved him "to infinity and beyond." Getting these matching tattoos on our shoulders also meant that we could then could bump arms in a ritual that could serve as a non-verbal gesture and sign of our special connection and solidarity. I agreed, even though the truth which I kept to myself then and he still doesn't even know today, is that even though we did watch the movie "Toy Story" fifty to a hundred times when he would come to my house, the statement "I love you to infinity and beyond" was never uttered once from my lips while he was growing up. In fact, it was a neighbor mom who would say that to her three daughters and Preston must have overheard it over the years. Didn't matter. He believed that "To infinity and beyond" was our saying, so that was the important thing. These matching shoulder tattoos were going to help get him home and give him a fighting chance to survive. Darnit, tattoos hurt. The pain of getting the tattoo was worth it though; this matching ink connection would serve us well for years to come. I even had my tattoo redone adding stars. The location of our matching tattoos on our shoulders is relatively prominent, so that either one of us can't help but be reminded of our familial bond on a daily basis.

So when a group of five people, all covered with tattoos, pulled up to my driveway on motorcycles displaying rainbow flags, I suspended any previously practiced judgement and welcomed them all to my garage sale with an open heart. I thought of them as "The Transgendered Tattoos." I knew that if my little Buzz Lightyear tattoo had such significance, that each one of their many tattoos most likely had tremendous meaning for them as well. My connection and kind acceptance of these garage sale shoppers turned out to be yet another extremely positive and transformative experience. Our shared interactions and conversations seemed almost Divine-driven and were filled with such unconditional love. Pure love. The feeling was sincerely overwhelming. I was reminded of the Oregon tattoo parlor owner Scrappy and the miracle moment when his observations, interjections and intervening shifted the course of my visit to save my nephew. My trip out West went from a pure act of love, support and concern to a real-life rescue mission. Preston has told me over and over again how very thankful he was that I followed my gut instinct and was given his dad's blessing to get to the Indianapolis International Airport, fly out to Oregon and search for him. He credits me for saving his life. I give credit to a power much greater and Divine than me. As the five Transgendered Tattoos were leaving my garage sale and heading away down the road from my house, I felt a Heavenly presence and love surrounded me with understanding and reassurance. Just then five very large red cardinals flew into my garage and circled me twice before heading out back into the sky. Was my brother Harold looking down on me in Spirit? Was Scrappy an Angel sent to protect Preston? Were the Transgendered Tattoos Angels? Were the five red cardinals a symbolic sign from Above? Did God come to my garage sale?

CHAPTER 9

Pennies from Heaven

"Instead of being afraid of death, we should try to awake to life; and the only death we should escape from is to forget the presence of God into us."

Laozi

I looked down from where I was sitting at my garage sale and saw one penny. The date on the coin was my birthday year. That was odd; it was odd enough that I made the effort to even look at the penny, let alone the date that was stamped on it. Throughout the garage sale I would also find pennies in other places. Normally I wouldn't think anything of it, but this was happening most every time I turned around, so I had no choice but to pay attention to them. I have heard that finding pennies and dimes, and other coins for that matter, indicate that someone from the Spirit world, either your deceased loved one or an Angel, is trying to communicate with you and get your attention. It is also confirmation for me that there are magical signs happening that just can't be explained in a logical, earthly manner. I have learned that our transitioned loved ones in Heaven actually want us to know that they are still part of our lives. I took the pennies as a sign that I was being blessed. Most everyone has heard the term "Pennies From Heaven" but probably don't know the history behind it. "Pennies From Heaven" was the title of a 1936 song with music by Arthur Johnston, lyrics by Johnny Burke and sung by Bing Crosby. I remember loving the "shoob doobie" touch to the beat of the song. There was also a film by the same name. Other famous musicians recorded the song, including Billy Holiday, Louis Armstrong, Tony Bennett, Frank Sinatra and Dean Martin. In the 1960s the song was a major hit when it was sung by the musical group The Skyliners. Andy Williams sang it, as did Regis Philbin; in fact the song was used as the soundtrack to Philbin's "Who Wants To Be A Millionaire" T.V. game show. As time went on the song continued its popularity with renditions from Paul Anka to Michael Buble. In 2016 Michael Keaton and Linda Cardellini performed a duet of the song for the film "The Founder." I was now starting to discover a more Spiritual meaning behind the term "Pennies From Heaven."

As a nurse, each year I would attend motivational seminars and staff development workshops given to help the medical professionals reach out to their younger patients with creative efforts. One idea I learned from a very thoughtful presenter included this "Champion Ring" concept. This nurse would have the young patient's family and friends write one positive statement about them on a separate notecard. The comments could be general like "you are funny" or they could be specific like "I like the way you are good about taking your medicine" or "Our family is so proud of how strong you are, even when you have to go to treatments at the doctor's office." Then the nurse would punch a hole in each card and fasten the set of cards to a large key ring calling it a "Champion Ring." As soon as the cards were collected she presented the young patient with their Champion Ring and told them that whenever they were ever feeling down they should pull out their Champion Ring and take a look at how valued they were by others. Well, I took this concept to a more personal level for my nephew Preston. With my brother's permission and access to his son's contacts on his phone and social media, I mailed out bright, fluorescent orange index notecards, with a pre-punched hole, to all of Preston's friends and family with instructions for them to write a favorite memory or draw a picture or add a photograph using both sides and then mail it back to me in the self-addressed stamped envelope I provided. When I had all of them returned to me, I found that I had collected over 100 cards. I took them to the local office supply store and had them laminated before making him his oversized Champion Ring. I presented this to Preston at his family birthday party and he absolutely loved it. This gesture was very time consuming, but a great deal of fun for me because it was a labor of love. As I was leaving his party I noticed a few pennies on the floor next to the exit. Then something unreal happened.

As I walked out of the party I felt a very strong, cool breeze on my face. This was the exact same breeze I had felt at my garage sale when I was thinking of the family tree books and reminiscing about my aunts. I looked down and found another penny. Before I could look at the date, I looked up and saw the outline of an extremely tall almost gargantuan figure of a person with enormous wings by its side. The wings were outlined in a bright, shimmering white light. I remember that I felt strong, supported and guided. You think I would be scared, but I wasn't. It's hard to put into words. I felt the breeze again and the figure was gone almost as fast as it had originally appeared. It's like I had time to acknowledge it and process the experience somewhat, but not fully. It left me questioning. Did I imagine this? I think this figure was an Angel and now it was gone. I didn't hear any voices, but I had a knowingness of gratitude. It felt as if I was being thanked from up Above for my efforts to help rescue my nephew Preston. I always felt a special bond with him which I'm sure was from the years of getting together with my brother Wade and watching him grow up. I am so glad that Preston trusted me enough to guide him out of such a critical, life-and-death drug situation when he was a lost soul out in Oregon. I'm so glad I babysat him all those times when he was younger. I'm even thankful that we watched "Toy Story" so many times and that he thought I would tell him that I loved him "to infinity and beyond," which ended up being the catalyst for the matching shoulder tattoos and my being able to get him back to Indiana to safety and rehab. Even though Preston struggled with addictions and wasn't always honest and forthcoming with his parents, he could count on love and support from his Aunt Janet.

Back to the reality of my garage sale. There was a young woman who was looking at the housewares section. Nestled among knick knacks, figurines and china was a collection of souvenir spoons. The first souvenir spoons in the United States were made of our Nation's capital in 1890 by Galt & Bros, Inc. and featured George Washington to mark the 100th year anniversary of his presidency. Collecting spoons became a popular hobby and was relatively inexpensive. I had collected spoons for my niece Sam ever since she was little. I would purchase a spoon every time I would visit a state on my many travels. When I was in Europe on trips, it was more difficult to find the traditional tourist spoon, even though the fad originated in Europe, so sometimes I would have to improvise and create a spoon to commemorate a particular locale. When Sam was young, she enjoyed knowing that this collection was for her. Her other aunt collected Lladro figurines for her, which were much nicer and more expensive, but she was never allowed to touch them because they could break, so she loved the spoons more. Sam would often be the one to start looking for spoons when she went on trips. She enjoyed the collection until she reached college age when she told me she thought collecting spoons was dumb. She said that she would rather have the money for new video games or clothes and asked if I could sell the collection at my garage sale, so I did. This young woman who was looking around my garage sale decided that she wanted to buy the collection to give to her mom, but all she had was change and wondered if she could give me the coins to hold all of the spoons until she could get to an ATM to withdraw more cash. I said that was no problem. She reached into her backpack and pulled out a gallon-sized bag of pennies! Was this a coincidence? Were the pennies sent by Spirits wanting to support me during this challenging time? Was this girl sent by the Heavens to give me some sort of sign that it was O. K. to let go of my niece's spoon collection? Were Spirits with me as I made Preston's Champion Ring? Were the pennies sent from Heaven? Did God come to my garage sale?

CHAPTER 10

Fiona's Feathers

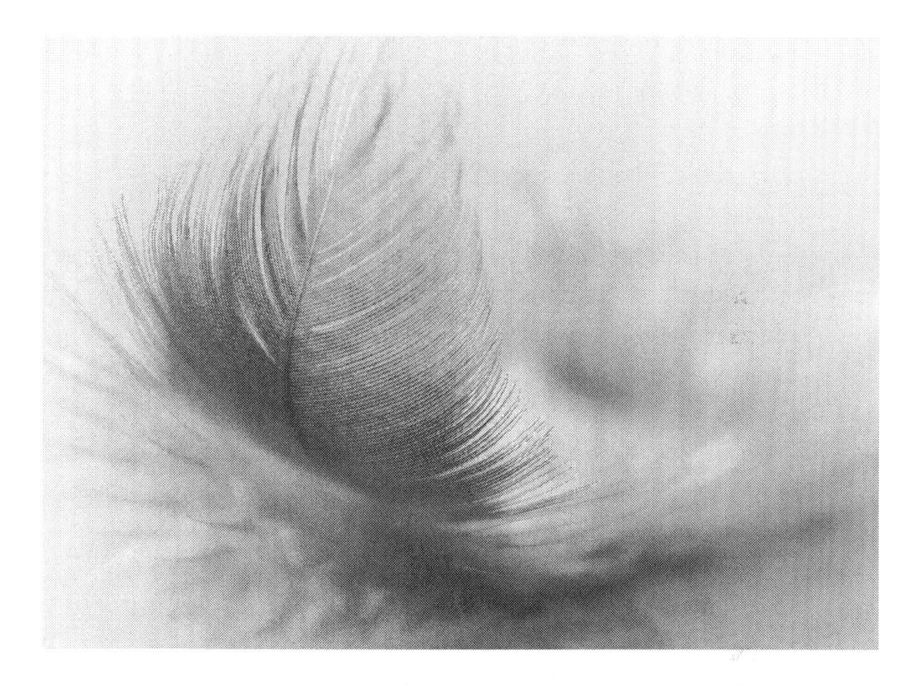

"We were born to make manifest the glory of God that is within us. It's not just in some of us. It's in everyone."

Nelson Mandela

A young man pulled up to the garage sale with three beautiful Australian Shepherd dogs, all on leashes. I instantly started to think about pets and how unconditional their love is. Dogs and cats and many other animals, because they don't have words or a brain that knows the human emotion of hate, make amazing companions for people. Their love and loyalty is consistent. I was "Aunt Janet" to my brother's dog Fiona. Fiona was Wade's fourth (and as he would always say "final") Australian

Shepherd. He would call her his "Little Aussie." These dogs were typically bred strictly for herding or show ring events, but many people have found they make awesome pets. Fiona was so smart and focused. She would tilt her head back and forth when you were talking as if she was really listening and understanding each word that was said. Wade would FaceTime me on the phone and show me Fiona's reaction when he would say, "Aunt Janet is coming over. She is bringing you a toy and a marrow bone." Fiona loved to learn tricks and loved all of the toys that I brought over, whether it was a flying disc, a ball or her favorite, a stuffed, furry squeaky rodent. She also waited with anticipation for me to reach into my pocket for the marrow bone I would always treat her to. Fiona was always so very active, so it was super hard to see her slow down at age 13, even though that is usually the last year of this breed's lifespan. Australian Shepherds have a very distinctive Merle coat. Their unique coloring includes dark blotches of fur against a lighter background of various earthy-toned colors, giving it a sort of marble appearance. Fiona had white markings and copper points around her face, ears and tail. Another striking feature is their range of eye colors: green, blue, brown, amber and hazel. Aussies can also have eyes that are different colors or even "split" eyes where half of the eye is one color and the other half is another color. Fiona had one eye that was blue and one eye that was brown. Wade got her as a puppy from a breeder for his son Preston. He knew to avoid the all-white Aussie because they are genetically predisposed to deafness and blindness. Fiona's coat was beautiful and had the distinctive fur coloring of black and amber.

Seeing this man with the Australian Shepherds reminded me of Fiona, my brother Wade's dog and a wonderful day at Wade's house when we were just hanging out in the backyard playing fetch with Fiona. We talked about fun things we did during our childhood in Brownsburg, a quaint upscale town in Hendricks County, Indiana. When my brother and I were in high school, the movie Hoosiers was filmed at the local gym and we both got to be extras on set, as did many other peers from Brownsburg High School or Harris Academy, the religious high school in town. We had a fun and free upbringing. We loved to go to this little hot dog stand called The Right Bank, which was the English translation of La Rive Droite. La Rive Droite is commonly associated with the northern side of the Seine River of central Paris, France in Europe. The Seine flows westwards and separates Paris into two when you are facing downstream. The Right Bank is also associated with places of sophisticated elegance because the most famous street on The Right Bank is the Champs-Elysees. There are other lesser known streets that are fancy-smancy such as Avenue Montaigne and Rue de la Paix-Rue de Rivoli. So instead of having this little everyday basic, Bohemian (Left Bank-Rive Gauche) hot dog stand, our hot dog stand was a bit upscale, servicing a more cosmopolitan clientele, hence the reason it was most likely named The Right Bank. The Right Bank is now owned by a high school classmate of mine who has chosen to keep the hot dog stand basically the exact same as it was when we grew up; so the Brownsburg Right Bank hot dog tradition continues. This classmate's family is into hot dog stands. His relatives are from Reykjavik, Iceland and hot dog stands are a big thing there. Since 1937 Reykjavík has been home to a small chain of hotdog stands called Baejarins Beztu Pylsur, although new vendors are trying to get in on the action. Hot dogs have become so famous in Iceland they are now mentioned in travel and tour guidebooks after former United States President Bill Clinton stopped by and had a hotdog while he was at a UNICEF conference in 2004. This hotdog chain has been known to sell over 1000 hotdogs in a day, especially since other celebrities have made a big deal about them including: The Kardashians, Ella Fitzgerald, the heavy metal band Metallica, Ben Stiller when he was filming the movie "The Secret Life of Walter Mitty" and of course, the cast of "Game of Thrones" since the series has many scenes filmed in Iceland. The Icelanders order these lamb hot dogs with everything including ketchup, sweet mustard, Remoulade (which is a mayonnaise-based condiment) and crisp fried and raw onion. They use the phrase "eina med ollu" which means "one with everything." The Right Bank is located on an alley just south of the town square. It is very nostalgic and still a popular hang out for students, even though the customers are new and much younger and don't have the familiar connection to it as my brother and I have. The building was founded in 1963 and was previously a barber shop. The hot dog stand was originally a push cart where the owner would sell hot dogs with all of the fixings at the town square on weekends. This was before fast food had its worldwide takeover. The seating consists of one long booth on one side and several small bistro tables with ice cream shoppe-like metal chairs on the other side. All lunches are still served on small plastic trays that have detailed little flowers on them.

My brother Wade and I always talked about what a hidden gem this hot dog stand was. For those of us who grew up frequenting it after school, The Right Bank was a childhood staple. Even to this day, if we ever go to our hometown, the first stop is to get a cheese dog with everything on it at The Right Bank. We go there, not just because we absolutely love the taste of the food (there are some unique tastes when it comes to Midwest hotdogs), but because it was a positive part of our nostalgic history, as were a few other establishments in town. The place looks exactly the same as it did when we were growing up and all through high school. It is a very simple and unique place that was painted a soft shade of lavender. The menu and the prices seemed to be the only things that have changed. I would and still always get the cheese dog with everything, which means ketchup, mustard, relish and onions with extra dill pickles on the side. My brothers Harold and Wade would also get the cheese dog, but they would have chili added on top. It would come with a bag of chips and a soft drink; all three of us would get root beers. Now the menu includes Frito Pie, Zucchini Chocolate Chip Muffins and gluten-free buns. Back when I was in high school, the in-crowd popular kids were invited to sit and eat their lunch in the back room. Of course, in high school I was not that lucky. As an adult though, I acted as if the back room was my usual spot, so I did eventually fulfill a childhood dream of eating my cheese dog with extra pickles in the back. Wade and I got to talking about our childhood. Our conversation turned to our late brother Harold. We were reminiscing about some fun times we had together, but mainly we talked about Harold's struggles with depression, addictions and gender identity, eventually contributing to his suicide. He left behind his wife Jane, who was also his best friend. Our family was shocked and grief stricken, but we had known that with Harold's emotional and physical challenges, suicide would be a possible outcome for him at some point in his life. Nevertheless, it was very painful news to hear and very sad for both Wade and myself. All of a sudden, the man at my garage sale who was walking around with three Australian Shepherds came up to me, told me that his name was Peter and that he was a psychic medium. He asked if I believed. I replied that I was most definitely open to whatever he had to say. Peter asked if the two of us could sit down and told me that there was already a man in his early 40's standing next to me. Wow. This was weird as Harold died in his early

40's and Wade and I were just talking about him. I didn't say anything, but I listened. I was getting a psychic medium reading at my garage sale!

Peter, this psychic medium, instructed me specifically to take three deep breaths to relax, told me again that there was a man standing behind me and to think about any young man close to me that had passed away. I took three deep breaths and my thoughts went right to my brother Harold, as I was just thinking about him and thinking about a conversation about Harold I just had with my brother Wade. Peter asked if I had a brother who had transitioned. I confirmed that one of my two brothers had passed away. He asked if my brother's name was Harold or Hank or some name that started with an H-a. I nodded. My jaw literally dropped as I couldn't believe he got my brother's name right away just as the psychic medium did at the IANDS reading. Oh my God! How could he know this? You can't make this stuff up. He didn't provide as much detail, but just to get his name was amazing.

There were more people approaching my driveway for the garage sale, so I knew I would have to tend to them. Besides, Peter said that my brother's Spirit was starting to leave him. He thanked me for my part in providing validation. Thanked me? It was the psychic medium that deserved all the thanks. As Peter was getting up to go, we both noticed this pile of bird feathers on the table. They didn't seem to be there before. We both commented on how unique these feathers were and that neither one of us had ever seen any feathers like this before; in fact, we had never even seen a bird with this type of split coloring of black and amber, almost like they were mimicking the colors of Australian Shepherds. Just then my cell phone rang. I answered it and it was Wade with some sad news. His beloved, well, our beloved Australian Shepherd Fiona had just that very moment peacefully passed away. I told this to Peter just as he was leaving. We both looked down at the table at the distinctively-colored feathers and Peter said that they were most definitely a sign from Heaven from Fiona. Was Peter the psychic medium and his Australian Shepherds sent to me so that I would think about Fiona and my brother Harold? Were those feathers sent from Fiona at the exact time of her death? Did Spirit have me reminisce about my childhood and favorite hot dog stand in Brownsburg? Did God come to my garage sale?

CHAPTER 11

Middletown, Marlene and Media

"Your talent is God's gift to you. What you do with it is your gift back to God."

Leo Buscaglia

The day before the garage sale, to reward myself for all my hard work the past month and just to feel better, I decided to treat myself to a mani-pedi at Fancy Nails just a couple of blocks away from my home in Westfield, Indiana. My nails were in bad shape because I had just spent the last two weeks going through boxes and getting ready for the garage sale. Prior to that I spent a good week scrubbing my friend Odetta's house after her passing from cancer. I was so distraught about her dying and still in shock that her health didn't improve and she was gone. She was on my mind when I went to the nail salon. You see, my friend Odetta fell ill on my birthday in October. We had just finished dinner at the local country club. The food at the restaurant was top notch, yet I remember Odetta not really eating much. I didn't think too much of that because she always ate small portions and was very finicky. As we were leaving the restaurant she had trouble standing up. The pain in her abdomen was sharp and heavy. She just sat and rested for a bit before attempting to get up and walk to the car. That night she ended up going to Riverview Health, Westfield Hospital's emergency room, for an evaluation. She was most definitely not a fan of Western medicine or hospitals; she was a devout patient of Dr. Wong, a Chinese herbalist in the southern suburbs. This holistic doctor had discouraged her from getting a colonoscopy and said that he personally didn't see the value in that test and doesn't get them himself. She heeded his example and recommendation, however at the ER an MRI and cat scan were ordered. The unfortunate thing was that only a partial image was done and that part came back clear. If the ER doctor would have ordered a full image, Odetta's colon cancer may have been detected and she would most likely be here on earth today. Dr. Wong should have been called Dr. Wrong for contributing to Odetta not getting the correct medical diagnosis and treatment.

Odetta left for one month of treatments in Los Angeles, California. While she was gone I tended to her Westfield house, collected and sorted her mail and did some major cleaning. I didn't want her to come home to piles and piles of dirty dishes, grimy floors, at least twenty loads of laundry and a complete domestic mess. It was clear that she must have been in survival mode, because picking up after herself before she left for the West Coast was not on her priority list. I remember cleaning her downstairs bathroom. I was amongst the organic and all-natural concoctions when I came across some products that were out of the ordinary for Odetta. Turns out she was a regular subscriber to a very expensive scheduled shipment program of Dr. Perricone's Anti-Aging creams. I knew these were the top-of-the-line in beauty products because I had seen them advertised before. Plus, my friend and next door neighbor Beth uses the entire line of Dr. Perricone's products and she only buys the best and most expensive creams and makeup in the beauty industry. Knowing that I probably shouldn't have, I opened one of the special night creams and took a big scoop and gently rubbed it on my face and neck. I felt a bit guilty, like I was doing something I clearly knew was wrong, but then I brushed off this feeling because I figured my friend Odetta would have wanted me to try these special creams, especially since she wasn't home or even well enough to use them herself right now. I remembered talking with her on the phone about what I should add to a care package box I was putting together to send out to her in L.A. That same day a brand new Dr. Perricone shipment was delivered to her doorstep. I thought that maybe having a new set of these luxurious products would make her feel better, so I asked if she would like me to add them to her package. She said that she would, so I included them, boxed everything up and headed to the post office. I got the call the next day that she had succumbed to her rapidly-spread colon cancer illness and had quietly passed away.

A part of me died that day. Although Odetta and I only knew each other a few years, we were very close. In fact, she would always refer to me as her "conjoined twin sister who was separated at birth." Our closeness seemed deeper than most friendships, as if we knew each other in a past life or something. I cared a lot about her. She appeared to care even more about me. She spent her time between two homes, one in Westfield in the Northwest suburbs of Indianapolis and the other in her hometown of Middletown, also in Indiana. She had always wanted for me to visit her in Middletown. One time, I had planned a road trip to go to Middletown for a few days, but the plans fell through for some reason. Odetta raised goats and was a dog breeder, in addition to being an amazing artist. She said she loved being in Middletown because the air was fresher, there were no chemicals used on her property, all of the animals could be free and healthy and she was more inspired to create her masterpieces. Someday I would make plans to go see her in her quaint hometown of Middletown. Even though I had already spent a great deal of time cleaning her home, now because she had unfortunately passed away, I wanted to make sure everything was really in order because I was sure that her family and friends would be coming by at some point to help sort and dispose of her belongings. I was already in purging mode because I was getting ready for my garage sale, so I kept the momentum going and did some deep cleaning at her house. I wanted her friends and family to just be able to focus on the important items of hers, not the stuff that was unnecessary. It was when I was done with the chores that I decided to treat myself to cleaning up my nails. I headed into town for a mani-pedi at Fancy Nails.

I was watching the T.V. while my feet were soaking in the hot, sudsy water. I have had pedicures at Fancy Nails before and they are such a treat. All of a sudden one of those never-ending, very busy infomercials came on. It really got my attention because it was for Dr. Perricone's beauty system and products. I had recently indulged in trying Odetta's cream and still felt a tad guilty about opening up the jar and using some without permission. I certainly was interested in what the advertisement had to say about it. I listened to the infomercial, but for some reason, time went by so very slowly. I felt glued to the T.V. for hours. I knew it was longer than most commercials as the announcer described and demonstrated each product that was included in the packaged set. I thought about Odetta. I again thought about how I had opened her Dr. Perricone cream, indulged and treated myself without permission. I reassured myself that I really didn't do anything wrong because, as it turned out, Odetta was now gone and would never had come home to use these products. I told myself that I really had nothing to feel guilty about. Time stood still. I couldn't take my eyes off of the T.V. I didn't even remember that I was in the middle of a pedicure. The Dr. Perricone infomercial finally came to an end and I saw that the next advertisement was starting. I kept my eyes fixated on the T.V. I was trying to figure out what product would be highlighted next, but it wasn't a product. It was a feature of sorts about the town of Middletown, Indiana. Middletown was Odetta's hometown, the place that I never made it to for a visit. I pictured in my mind's eye Odetta's simple white house on top of a hill surrounded by nature and far away from civilization. I remembered that Odetta would say that it was the best place for an artist to live. She loved to paint in Middletown. She said she felt so connected to the natural world when she was there. Her animals would run free on the property, unlike their caged-existence at her other home in the suburb of Westfield. The Middletown commercial was running, but my mind was wandering; I was thinking fondly of Odetta and her life.

The last few years Odetta also got into photography. She would take numerous photos around dusk and into the evening, that when developed later showed hundreds of outstanding and unique orbs. These orbs came in all shapes and sizes and colors. Most of these orbs had either a person's or an animal's face smack dab in the center. They were mind-boggling to see. She would show me her photographs and we would really study the faces. The faces were so clear that there was no question what or who they were; it wasn't just a case of my brain playing tricks on me making me see something that really wasn't there. The faces in the orbs were so distinct that there was no way they could be be attributed to moisture or water droplets on the camera lens. I didn't know much about orbs, but had heard that there was a debate on whether orbs actually contain the energy of Spirits of loved ones that have passed on. That is what Odetta believed. She bought a large quality printer so she could use oversized paper to print her revealing orb photographs. She devoted time to her orb photographs as she continued her painting and caring for her animals. My attention returned to the T.V. and I was drawn back into the segment on Middletown. It really wasn't a commercial or a documentary, in fact, I couldn't really make sense of the purpose of this programming, so specific to this town with no real theme. I know I've mentioned this before, but time really slowed down. I even felt time in the air and it was thick and heavy. I couldn't take my eyes off the screen. I listened to the narrator talk about this Americana town in Central Indiana. The name of the town was clearly typed in at the lower right-hand corner of the T.V. screen: Middletown, Indiana. I remember thinking that it was so odd to have a commercial on a town. I knew that was the name of Odetta's town, but the impact of the significance didn't fully register with me yet. Why would this town be highlighted on T. V.? I kept watching. The video on the screen switched perspectives and was now an aerial view of the Main Street in Middletown probably taken by someone using a drone. I had never seen this particular town, so this was the first time I got an idea of what it looked like. Then this view changed and the camera was focused on an old woman with short, curly, white hair. She was sitting on the back of an ambulance and she was smiling as she talked about the wonderful emergency and responder services that the town of Middletown has for its community members, especially the elderly. I began thinking that maybe this was an infomercial on the ambulance service company. Just like the Dr. Perricone segment, time seemed to stand still and this Middletown ad went on for hours. I felt like I was in a trance when the Fancy Nails nail tech asked me what color nail polish I would like to use on my toes. So, wait a minute here, she is just now getting to my toes? I felt like I had been in the nail salon for the entire day. I remembered that when I started the pedicure that was when the Dr. Perricone infomercial started. That went on forever, as did this current segment (I'm not sure really what to call it-commercial, documentary or highlight) on Middletown, Indiana, yet in reality not much time did go by if the nail tech was just now getting to painting my toenails. I've had pedicures before and even the longest one I have ever had only took 20 minutes at most. I was confused and in a fog, but it didn't even occur to me to talk with anyone or ask any questions. I felt like I had just experienced something life altering, yet I didn't have the desire or energy to think about it deeper. I should have asked the ladies getting pedicures next to me if they were seeing the same things I saw on the T.V., but I didn't. Did they see the Perricone infomercial? Was it super long? Did they witness the Middletown, Indiana segment with the old lady and the ambulance?

The garage sale was now over and a month passed before I had a fleeting thought about my experience at Fancy Nails. It was almost as if what I saw and what I went through was suppressed deep within me. Why did it start to resurface now? I decided to really rack my brain and try to remember the details of my experience. I was with Odetta's family in her Westfield, Indiana home going through photographs when I came across a few pictures of this elderly lady. To my surprise, this lady was the exact spitting image of the lady that I saw on the nail salon T.V. during that long, long segment on Middletown. I remember seeing this elderly woman sitting on the back of an ambulance, and here she was in Odetta's photographs. I asked Odetta's family her name and who she was. Her family told me that her name was Marlene and she was a very, very close friend of Odetta's from Middletown; in fact she named her favorite goat after her. Odetta considered Marlene family. The only biological family that lived in the same state as Odetta was her brother and his wife, both of whom she didn't respect or keep in contact with. Marlene was close to 100 years young. She was definitely the exact same lady that I saw sitting on the back of the ambulance as I watched some sort of documentary or commercial on Middletown that day when I had that unusual experience while getting a pedicure. I shared this with Odetta's family and a couple of friends of mine, but nobody seemed to care or think anything was unusual.

I guess you've got to be discerning regarding who you talk with about this Spiritual stuff; not everyone is interested, believes or even gets it.

I've read that departed souls can communicate through electronic technology. Lights can flicker on and off, music can start playing on an unplugged radio, voices can be recorded on tape players, so why couldn't someone who has passed away communicate using a television? After seeing Marlene's photograph, I thought about and remembered the fact that I saw an aerial shot of the Main Street of Middletown on the same program, so I decided to Google an image of Middletown, Indiana, just to see if there was any resemblance of what I saw on the screen and the reality of what the town really looked like. OMG!!! The image I researched on the computer was the exact image I saw on the T.V. screen at the Fancy Nails salon! There was no question in my mind. Now this was crazy. I didn't have an NDE, but I certainly believe that I had experienced the next best thing. I think it is called an STE: a Spiritually Transformative Encounter. After everything I went through with this experience, I believe that my friend Odetta contacted me from another energy plane. She got my attention from the Dr. Perricone beauty products. Nobody knew about my using her face cream that day. It had to be Odetta that kept my attention for God only knows how long, because time literally stood still enough for her to show me her hometown in Middletown, Indiana. I had never met Marlene, but because Marlene was important to Odetta, she made sure that I got to see who she was. In fact, I know this sounds weird, but if Marlene was Odetta's soul-sister and I was also Odetta's soul-sister, than that would mean that Marlene and I are soul-sisters as well. Something Divine, maybe God, most-definitely had his hand in this life-altering experience. Was my trying the Dr. Perricone cream and then later seeing an infomercial coincidental? Did Odetta and Marlene come to my garage sale? Were there Spirits at work while I was getting my nails done at the salon? Was Marlene really in an infomercial about Odetta's hometown of Middletown? Can Spirits come through electronics? Did God came to my garage sale?

CHAPTER 12

Nathan's Repeating Numbers

"We are seen in all our need. We will be heard. We can believe. One by one we are a chain that brings us back to love again. Love is grace that lets us be forgiven and completely free. Good prevails and hope is true. God's favorite miracle is you."

Livingston Taylor

I met Nathan during my freshman year of college. We weren't attracted to each other romantically, or at least I wasn't, but a nice and caring platonic friendship ensued. Nathan was a bit of a loner and didn't socialize a lot. He was the youngest of three siblings who were all a year apart and were also attending the same college. His older brother and sister were much more outgoing, as I was. Nathan and I applied for and got part-time jobs as lifeguards at the college pool. There were always two lifeguards assigned at a time and we often found ourselves working the same shifts. Also, the pool wasn't used very much during the student open-swim times, so we had a lot of time to sit, chat and get to know one another. Nathan was a math major and was fascinated by numbers. I distinctly remember him telling me that he would regularly come across certain repetitive numbers and really believed that there was some Spiritual or mystical reason that these numbers would appear to him when they did. He said he would be drawn to look at the clock or his watch at 11:11, whether it was in the morning or evening. His birthday was also November 11 and he would tell me that he couldn't wait until his "Triple Golden" birthday on November 11, 2011. I had heard of Golden Birthdays when the date of your birth matches your age; that would mean Nathan had already had his Golden birthday when he turned 11 years old. So, I guess what he meant by his "Triple Golden Birthday"' would be the day he turned 33 years old. Unfortunately he didn't live long enough to experience that special birthday. I finally was able to sit down for a few moments because currently there were no garage sale customers. I checked my watch and surprisingly the time was 11:11, so naturally I thought of Nathan. Just as my mind turned to thoughts of Nathan, the song that I associated with him, the song that we would call "ours," came on the radio. Nathan and I would always listen to a musical folk group duo named England Dan and John Ford Coley. We loved their mellow harmonies and simple, yet heartfelt lyrics. Our song was called "Love Is The Answer." This soft rock song was written by Todd Rundgren for his band Utopia. I can't believe that our song came on at exactly 11:11. It surely seemed like a coincidence, but then, as I'm coming to find out, there are really no such things as coincidences. Often times, what we think of as a coincidence is really a synchronicity and one of Spirit's ways of communicating with us to let us know that they are guiding us with love. Nathan was a guy that I connected with more on a soul level than anything else.

Thinking back to before I went to college, I was a very outgoing high school student; I was focused, fun and positive and I was open to establishing new friendships. I was involved in high school extracurricular activities like Field Hockey, Madrigal Singers, Cheerleading, Talent Show, Student Council, Musicals, Service Club and the school newspaper. Throughout my three years in high school (I graduated early) I enjoyed life. I held two jobs to pay for my own clothes. I had a great boyfriend who was a year ahead of me in school. I got along with students in all of the different high school social cliques and groups: the jocks, the burnouts, the rah-rahs, the dramatics and the band geeks. Every era has basically the same breakdown of coteries, they are just called different names. I just missed the generation of high school students with groups named the dupers (penny loafer, blue jean wearing everyday kids), the greasers (the smoking hard-asses with the leather jackets and greased hair), the collegiates (college-bound preppy academics), the hippies (counter-culture flower children who tout peace, love and nonviolence), the weekend hippies (normal during the week and who let loose on Saturdays and Sundays), the nerd cases (theatre, music), the super brainiacs (Ivy League-ers), the jocks (athletes) and the cheerleaders. Nowadays high school students have groups called the popular kids (athletes and cheerleaders), emos (emotional gothics), gang members (dangerous bad guys) and drug dealers (self-explanatory), nerds (smart kids that like school), band nerds (nerds that play musical instruments), the theatre kids, the LGBTQs and Transgenders and the geeks (the anti-social loners). Two weeks before my high school boyfriend's graduation I got it in my head that maybe I could graduate too and move on with my life (and away from Brownsburg, Indiana and from the constraints of home). I was 15 years old in my junior year and never had previously given early graduation a thought. I asked my guidance counselor if this was a possibility and sure enough, after a quick review of my transcript, I was told I had enough credits to graduate early if I wanted to. So I did. If I would have thought about it and reflected on the decision a bit more, I may have stayed for my senior year because not only would I have been an extra in yet another blockbuster movie with my class, but I would have been able to go on the senior trip to Europe. Oh well. I chose to charge ahead with my life. Where were my parents while I was making this decision? I don't remember their involvement or input. I guess I was left on my own to chart my own course. My high school boyfriend and I never even entertained the thought of continuing our relationship after high school, so that was not a factor in my decision to graduate early. We both graduated high school and lovingly parted ways as we each marched on different paths following the beats of our different drummers.

Nathan was one of the first people I met during my freshman college orientation. Somehow we felt so comfortable with each other and became fast friends right from the get go. We both commented that we must have known each other in a previous life or something because of the ease in our connection. I never really believed in that stuff, you know, previous lives and all. I do now; I've had too much proof to discount the reality of it. So, I'm sitting here at my garage sale thinking of Nathan at 11:11 A. M. as our song comes on. Then I heard a voice. I literally heard someone talking to me. There was nobody there, but the voice was clear, low and very masculine. There was a strange deepness to the voice, unlike anyone's voice I had ever heard before. He said, "Hey there, you are finally paying attention to me." I didn't know what to think. I looked around again, but nobody was there. I was seriously all alone at my garage sale, or so I thought. Could the voice be Nathan's? I know Nathan loved me as a friend. Nothing more. Well, looking back he may have held a spark of romantic interest at one point, but if so it was nothing that he followed through with or told me about. Maybe he sensed that my feelings for him were solely on a platonic friendship level and took his cue from that. The significant connection was there though. I believed and verbalized to Nathan and others that I was an Atheist, like my parents, who did not believe in God or any other type of higher power. My dad and mom did not partake in any form of organized religion, so neither did I. When Nathan and I would be engrossed in one of our long philosophical discussions, somehow the topic always led to God and Nathan's strong belief that God, Angels and Spirits were watching over us. He believed we humans all had a time to live and a time to die. Nathan loved talking with me. It seemed so many of our other classmates avoided him and didn't develop a relationship with him because of a very odd and awkward physical characteristic of his. Nathan had a trait, I guess you would call it, that I knew was present, but I chose to overlook, so it didn't factor into my view or acceptance of him. This is uncomfortable to discuss, but here goes. There was something in Nathan's anatomy and clothing style that contributed to people feeling uncomfortable being around him. This led to Nathan being somewhat isolated. He never seemed to even know that something was amiss and quite different or noticeable. Nobody, not even me, felt comfortable talking to him about it. You see, Nathan would wear extremely tight jeans. These jeans were noticeable enough because they seemed way too small and snug for him; people would call his pants "clam diggers." But that wasn't the biggest issue. The crotch area around his zipper bulged out to the point of even making his jean's fly zipper stretch. In fact it looked like there was a small pillow stuffed in there. People would talk behind his back about his "pouch" from time to time. Nathan had no idea. If he did, he may have bought larger pants. I'm surprised that his brother and sister, who were also at the same school, didn't say anything to him. I really don't think Nathan had a clue that his bulging jeans were a topic of this small college gossip mill. I knew of it and saw it, but it never really was an issue for me. Certainly it was nothing I ever felt the need to bring to his attention. As I've said before, I have always thought of myself as an open minded, non-judgemental, accepting person. I look at someone's heart and personality and don't let appearances sway my opinion of them. I heard the voice again; this is the same low voice that spoke to me right after I noticed the clock strike 11:11 and our song came on. This time the voice said "Thank you for your love." I started to wonder if it somehow was Nathan in Spirit speaking to me from across dimensions. You see, Nathan died. Nathan had tragically lost his life in a car accident. According to his older sister, who had phoned me to break the terrible news, Nathan was driving along a quiet stretch of road as he was coming home from a friend's house. He fell asleep at the wheel, lost control of his car, hit a tree head-on and was killed instantly. I remember his sister making a big deal that Nathan's accident happened at 11:11 P. M. which were the numbers of his birthday, November 11th. As you can imagine, I was devastated by this news. I was so thankful that his sister had my phone number; Nathan must have kept it among his personal belongings. His sister knew we were friends. I continued to communicate and exchange letters (there was no texting or cell phones back then) with Nathan's sister for around four years after his death. I think we provided reciprocal healing for each other to help us each cope with Nathan's death and our grief. Nathan was the first close friend that I knew pass away. There was only one other contemporary I knew that died. There was a girl named Betty that died when I was in high school; she was actually murdered and it shook our school and small Indiana town to its core.

Betty was a beautifully vivacious girl. We were in the same year and had many classes together, but we didn't hang out in the same social circles, so we never got to know one another really well. Betty was fairly popular, but unlike the aloof Rah-Rahs, she seemed to be a real down-to-earth, nice and friendly person. After her murder, our classmates talked about the tragedy for the entire time we were in high school. It was often said that Betty was actually overly-nice and overly-approachable and that those traits played a role in her fate. Some even verbalized that she "deserved what she got" because she wore very revealing and slim-fitting dresses, accentuating her breasts and perfect figure. To me those comments were not only wrong, they were disgusting; nobody deserves to be murdered and how people dress doesn't cause or justify someone murdering them. As I was sitting at my garage sale, I went back into the house to find my high school yearbook. I pulled out the local newspaper clipping from Betty's murder to look over what was said about her. It had been years since I looked at it, but I knew I had kept it stashed away. I saw that the date of her death was November 11th. Another 11-11 sign. Was the universe trying to get my attention? How odd that I would be sitting here thinking about two young people I knew that had both died and they both were very strongly and unmistakably connected to the repeating numbers 11-11.

Betty had driven to meet friends at a bar just over the state line. Back then the drinking age in Indiana was 21, but the neighboring state was still 18. So, it was a regular occurrence for the older high schoolers to drive 45 minutes or so to a disco bar just over the state line to partake in some "slamming of brewskies" as the cool kids would say. Well, our beautiful classmate Betty, I'm sure, being her nice and friendly self, talked with guys at the bar. Unfortunately, she ended up being followed home by some deranged townie thug. Later it was revealed by her friends who were with her that night that Betty had very politely refused the townie's advances at the disco bar. The next morning Betty was missing, but her purse and all of its contents were strewn about her family's well-manicured front lawn leading authorizes to suspect that there was foul play. After a few days of searching, Betty's nude and raped body was discovered in a shallow grave in the backyard of some guy's house. Betty's clothes were found bunched up under the front porch. Oh my God! This kind of thing never ever happened to anyone from our town. You wouldn't even hear about a murder like this in the news because this kind of thing rarely happened back then anywhere, at least not in Midwest suburbia. What a shock to our entire school and community. Just then, as I was sitting at my garage sale, I thought to myself, quietly without spoken words, "Betty, my thoughts and prayers go out to you and your family, especially your parents. They have had to endure the loss of you, their daughter, and as I later learned your older brother died 15 years after you. May you both Rest In Peace." I didn't realize that there was a young lady standing over me wanting to pay for a $12.00 item. She told me that she only had $11.11 and wondered if I would accept that instead of $12.00. Another number sign!

I thought back to Nathan's repeating numbers and the song we agreed was "ours." I realized that the song lyrics almost gave me a warning about his death. The lyrics to the England Dan and John Ford Coley song "Love Is The Answer" are as follows: "Who knows why. Someday we all must die. We're all homeless boys and girls. And we are never heard. Tell me, are we alive, or just a dying planet? When you're near the end, love one another." Immediately after hearing the song I was thinking of each word to our song and analyzing the significance that I now realize. Then I heard that voice again. "I'm here. I'm always with you." Just then I saw Nathan's face about two or three inches away from my face. There was no neck or body, just his face. His face was outlined in a golden white luminescence. It was almost like his face was somehow projected into the air electronically. It reminded me of the audiovisual effect of the super-sized face of the Wizard from a scene in the classic movie (one of my favorites) "The Wizard of Oz." This was where Dorothy and her compadres mustered up all of their collective braveness to see the Wizard in the Emerald City and without looking behind the curtain they asked for help with their wish for Dorothy to return back home to Kansas. The Wizard's face was projected onto the curtain as he told Dorothy, the Scarecrow, the Tin Man and the Lion ("and Toto too") that in order for their wish to be granted, they would first need to return with the broom from the Wicked Witch of the West. Nathan's face was most definitely of his image, but it sure had a resemblance to the effects of the Wizard in that scene of the movie.

I communicated without words, just thoughts in my head, "Nathan, I miss you. You meant a lot to me dear friend. I now know that I meant a lot to you as well. I realize that there is a major significance to the numbers 11-11. Thank you for visiting me today. Thank you for leading me to think of my high school classmate Betty. Thank you for showing me that there is more to this life on earth than it appears. Thank you for reminding me of our connection on earth and now with you in Spirit." Did Angels have a hand in my meeting Nathan in college? Did Nathan's Spirit come to my garage sale? Was his projected face real? Did Betty, my high school classmate's Spirit come to my garage sale? Were the numbers 11-11 a sign from above? Did God come to my garage sale?

CHAPTER 13

The Sari and The Dream Visitation

"Do not fret, for God did not create us to abandon us."

Michelangelo

During the second and final day of the garage sale my coworker friend Renee stopped by with her 25 year old daughter Jan. Renee knew I had to unload most of my furniture. Her daughter had just purchased a condo on River Avenue in an upscale Indianapolis neighborhood and needed to furnish it. Renee also knew that I would never charge her for anything. Even though I really needed the money because of my decision to go solo resulting in my being financially devastated, I would never charge a friend for anything and would be uncomfortable asking for or accepting any money. Her daughter picked out a dresser, a couple of end tables with matching lamps and a beautiful Persian-inspired synthetic rug. I would have kept the rug if it didn't sell, but I had to let it go because Jan really wanted it. Oh well. The reassuring affirmation I found myself saying a lot was that even if I didn't recoup much (or any) money, I needed to get rid of things, so anything that left my garage sale was a blessing and would help me move onto the next phase of my life, a phase where the emphasis was no longer on creating a beautifully decorated home or the accumulation of household goods, but more on simplicity and only owning what I needed and could use. Jan found other items and made a pile near where I was sitting in a lawn chair. One of the items she chose was a Sari that I have held onto my entire life. She said she liked this fabric as it reminded her of when she visited India. Just then I heard a voice say "No" and I somehow realized that I could not part with the Sari and promptly removed it from her pile. Jan had loved items from all over the world. She wanted to serve in the Peace Corp in India, but in the fall of 1976 the Peace Corp was phased out of that country, mostly because the Pakistani-Bangladesh Civil War of 1971 and then Secretary of State Henry Kissinger's accepting the Indian Prime Minister Indira Gandhi's choice not to request any more volunteers. Jan knew that she wanted to serve somewhere in the Middle East. She was very excited to work and live on the south end of Settat, Morocco. She liked that it was only a couple of hours away from the long plateau to Marrakesh. When she talked about it, I could hear the Crosby, Stills and Nash song "Marrakesh Express" playing in my head, which was a song that was popular in the early 1970's. It was clear that Jan had an affinity and appreciation for more culturally diverse decor. Even her clothing had a Bohemian-Boho style to it. At first I didn't say anything about the Sari, but after hearing the voice say "No" and listening to my gut and intuition, I knew I couldn't part with this ornate and oversized piece of cloth. I knew that this Sari held some sort of an amazing significance and that I should keep it. The voice said again "Save the Sari" three times. I looked around and nobody was there who would say anything like that. I told Jan that I really needed to keep the Sari and she was very cool about it and didn't give it another thought. I felt like an Indian-giver (no inaccurate pun intended) which was not usually anything I would ever do. I took the Sari and ran it into the house so that it wouldn't be sold by mistake. I remember thinking how strange it was that I heard a voice telling me to keep the Sari. I tried to rationalize it by saying that I was just talking to myself, but I know I wasn't. I really heard a voice command to me, not just once but three times in a row. It reminded me of Lawrence Kasdan's 1991 star-studded movie "Grand Canyon" where fate and happenstance along with the possibility of God and grace were interwoven into the fabric of a particular scene. There was one part in the movie where the character Claire, played by Mary McDonnell, finds an abandoned baby while she is out for a jog. She had been longing to have or care for a child and then this miracle event happened and presented itself in a split second. As she was jogging she heard a voice coming from an old homeless man say "Keep the baby." In the movie it sounded like the same voice I heard with "Keep the Sari."

The Sari from India, made from vintage silk, was something I know now that I was not supposed to unload at my garage sale. My mom told me it was given to her from a man she knew and was close to in graduate school when they both were earning their Master's degrees. I remember her telling me that real gold threads were woven into the edges of the Sari. I know it must have had some major sentimental value to her because she held onto it for so many years and passed it down to me. Women's saris are garments worn by women that are several yards long and made of thin, decorative fabric. They are wrapped in a traditional way and draped around one shoulder. The most common fashion, the Nivi style, originated in Andhra Pradesh, India. The word "Sari" in Sanskrit means "Strip of cloth." This garment can be traced back to 2800-1800 BC to the Indus Valley Civilization. My mom's Sari was made of vintage silk with gold thread, however natural plant dyes were used for the colors. In the 5th millennium BC dyes were made from indigo, lac, red madder and turmeric and these substances can still be found used today to dye Saris. I had no idea that this Sari would make such an impact on my life at my garage sale just with hearing a voice. I had a trip planned to India and part of the itinerary included visiting this man, my mom's old love who was now in his 80s and who gave my mom this Sari. I had no idea that their relationship was actually a unique love affair that crossed cultural, political and societal lines. Theirs was a love story that defied all odds and was pure and true. They did not care that their skin colors were different or that they practiced different religions or came from different cultures or were separated by legal borders or an expansive ocean. They could never see their love affair through because of society's mores and laws that pulled on and separated their heartstrings. They eventually and reluctantly went along with their respective cultural dos and don'ts and shouldas over the natural connection of the love that they shared.

One evening I decided to search for more stuff to sell at my garage sale in the nooks and crannies of this beautiful house I had to leave. I had to abandon my digs, which meant I had to clean out every area of the house possible. I needed to see if there were any other items I could salvage to add to the garage sale. I went into the crawl space where I stored stacks of collected newspapers from important historical, social or sporting headlines and stories. Even though we lived in Indiana, my children worshipped the athletically talented superstar Michael Jordan and followed the Chicago Bulls when they won the basketball championships in the 1990s and were hailed as the NBA's greatest dynasty with two three-peats. Also in the pile were newspapers from Osama bin Laden's eradication in 2011 at a compound in AbboHabad on the orders of U.S. President Barack Obama and his "War on Terror." As I was looking around the crawl space, I came across a sturdy red Marshall Field's box (before the Chicago department store was acquired by Macy's in 2005) that had a yellow cut-out star with my name on it. I knew the label was in my dad's writing, so it must have been a box of things he saved and wanted me to have; I just didn't remember it. I had no idea that when I opened the box up the contents would change the course of my life and my future travels. When I took the lid off and peered inside, I was amazed to find it filled with old, onion-skinned, par-avion international stationary; this was the kind of paper that was cut out in a particular shape with flaps that when you fold in a certain way, the letter turned into a built-in envelope. This stationary was even pre-stamped. In the box were all these hand-written letters addressed to my late mother. The letters were all from India and they were love letters from the man that gave my mom the Sari. I spent the next six hours in the crawl space very gingerly opening the fragile letters, reading and rereading each one. I was so surprised that my dad saved these for me: love letters to my mom from another serious relationship that started before my parents' 1960 wedding. Time, again, actually stood still as I perused the emotionally-laden correspondence. I felt as if I was in a time warp because I really didn't have a sense of how many hours that seemed to effortlessly pass by. I thought about how communication differs so much from that time and era in history to this time in present day. We currently live in an age of instant communication. Heck, you could post a photo of yourself on Facebook, Instagram, Twitter or Snapchat and within minutes it can instantaneously reach thousands of people worldwide. Back when my mom received these letters, there was so much time invested in writing, sending and waiting for letters. Phoning someone out of the country was just not done due to the high cost. In fact, back when I was younger we didn't even want to waste a dime making a phone call from a local phone booth. When I was in middle school and went into town for the movies, I remember our family's phone protocol: I would put a dime in the payphone and call the operator to place a collect call to my parents. They would not accept the call and that would be my parents' cue to come pick me up. I would hang up the receiver and would be able to save the dime for next time. I grew up learning many ways from my parents on how to save money. One of the biggest memories of them saving money was that during my entire childhood, my parents would split a half gallon of milk into two containers and then they would make Sanalac from water mixed with powdered milk to fill up the remaining half in each container. I learned to be very careful with money. How odd it would be that in my adult life I would end up bankrupt, financially destitute and having to leave my foreclosed home even though I worked hard my entire life and contributed all of my money and savings to our family and this home.

With these discovered love letters, the wait and anticipation of it all most likely contributed to the fond memories and longing that people had for each other; this is something that is rarely experienced in today's modern world. This era of letters and letter writing was brought to the big screen in the famous romantic 2004 drama movie "The Notebook," directed by Nick Cassavetes and written by Jeremy Leven from Jan Sardi's adaption of the 1996 novel by Nicholas Sparks. The film stars the young Rachel McAdams and Ryan Gosling and the older Gina Rowlands and James Garner who fall in love in the 1940's, but are separated by war and class differences. As they age and the wife succumbs to Alzheimer's disease, the husband reads to her daily from a notebook of love letters describing their love. I could feel my mom's presence around me. Although she had passed away in 1996 and couldn't possibly be with me in physical form, I just knew she was with me in Spirit. I guess at this point in my experiential mystical journey I shouldn't question this. I'm now learning about NDEs and STEs that prove that we do not really die. I now regularly attend monthly IANDS meetings, watch a lot of YouTube testimonials and participate in individual and group psychic medium readings. Actually, because of my recent Awakening I am much more in tune to the possibility of the Spiritual and energy realms of consciousness. I have opened up my awareness, some would say my third eye, which has led me to a newfound life-altering view of our earthly existence and our limited human experience. My Awakening has led me to experience firsthand the testimonials of people's brushes with the Afterlife. There are many authentic and credible individuals that I have heard speak including scientists and everyday people that were non-believers until they themselves had a Spiritual experience and Awakening. Nowadays, often for a hefty fee, you can book your own individual reading from one of the many world-renowned evidential psychic mediums across the country and abroad. As with anything, there will always be individuals that tout that many who proclaim they are gifted with the ability to talk with the dead, are actually charlatans. It's true; there are some people who claim they have exceptional abilities even though they don't.

After my garage sale was over I was exhausted. Even though I had sold a huge amount of items, including the bulky furniture that would be hard to otherwise dispose of, I still had many items to pack up. Most of the leftovers went to piles for various charity pick ups. I did have some items, although they were slated for the garage sale because I had determined that I couldn't use them or didn't want them, that I still had a hard time just giving away, so I boxed those items up to rethink what I wanted to do with them. I finally was able to crawl into bed. I looked at the clock and it was exactly 11:11 P.M. While I was sleeping, I had a dream that felt so very real. I am a big dreamer. I dream in color and am often visiting lands that I have never seen before. I almost suppressed this, but as a child and throughout my young adult life I experienced was is termed "xenoglossy."

I had the ability, when I was dreaming, to speak a foreign language and even a few different languages to which I was never exposed to. My parents, brothers, college roommates and family would be amazed to hear me as I slept because the foreign words uttered from my mouth seemed so authentic. Well, this night, the night when my garage sale was over, I had a visitation from my mom. She was not as I expected her to be. She appeared to present herself from the time she was in graduate school and in love with this classmate, the man from India who gave her the sari. I have heard it said that when the Spirit of a deceased loved one visits you that they can choose how they want to look and how old they are. My mom, most likely because of my sari experience and my finding her India love letters, chose to come to me as a young woman during that time. I remember thinking that this was not a dream, but knowing it was a real live visit. I didn't try to reach out to touch her, but I distinctly remember that if I did, I would be able to feel her as if she were physically with me in flesh and blood. She was dressed in very tight, black stirrup pants that were high-waisted with a taper to the ankle. She had on a pullover knit striped turtleneck. Her hair was in a short bobbed style and she donned a stretchy headband. My mom had on Mary Jane strap shoes and was lying on my bed. She was on her stomach with her legs bent at the knees. Her ankles were crossed and she was just smiling at me. She didn't say a word, but neither did I. I was filled with such a warm, loving feeling from seeing my mom. It was almost like she was confirming that I did the right thing in keeping the sari; I felt her giving me thanks for honoring her with my thoughts of love for her and interest in her life back when she was in love with this man from India. Yep, I know now that I most definitely had a dream visitation. I also felt the reassurance from her that despite losing my home and financial security, prompting me to have this life-altering garage sale, that I would be alright. I would not only survive this life change, but I would thrive. This turning point in my life would be the catalyst for my Spiritual Awakening.

I have heard it said by many who have devoted their earthly lives to developing their intuition, that we are Spiritual beings having an earthly, human experience. So, if that is true, that would mean that the sari experience I had at my garage sale where I heard a voice telling me to "Keep the Sari," along with the unbelievable feeling of my mom's presence in an actual dream visitation from her, were truly Divine communications from the Spirit world that were directed at me to give me guidance and awareness. Was it a coincidence that my coworker Renee and her daughter Jan who wanted my mom's sari came to the garage sale? Was the sari saved for all those years just to reappear at my garage sale part of a Divine intervention? Did my Atheist dad who saved my mom's India love letters know that his actions would contribute to my Spiritual evolving? Did my mom really visit with me in a dream providing me love and support from another dimension? Did God come to my garage sale?

Yes, I do believe that God Came To My Garage Sale.

THE END

Made in the USA
Middletown, DE
19 January 2021